The

Seven Hindu Spiritual Laws

The
Seven Hindu Spiritual Laws

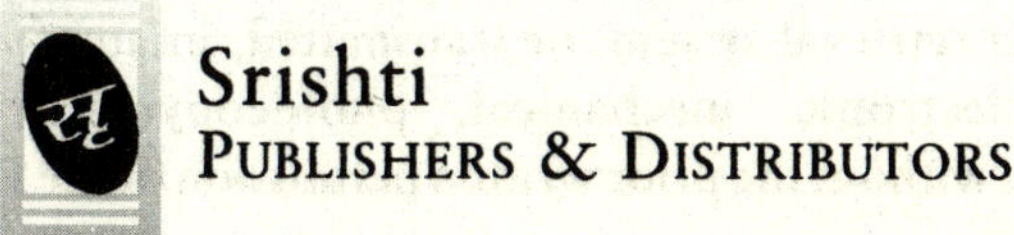

SRISHTI PUBLISHERS & DISTRIBUTORS
N-16, C. R. Park
New Delhi 110 019
srishtipublishers@gmail.com

First published by Srishti Publishers & Distributors 2004

This impression 2011

Cover design by Creative Concept

Typeset in AGaramond 11pt. by Suresh Kumar Sharma at Srishti

This edition is only for sale in India, Pakistan, Srilanka, Bangladesh and Nepal.

Printed and bound in India

Contents

Seven Hindu Spiritual Laws

The Law of Brahman

Every individual is a
Field of Infinite Potentiality
seeking "Self" expression –
which is possible only through
altruistic, desire-fulfilling activities.

The Law of Maya

Change is a tool of Brahman's expression.
The phenomenal world is always in flux.
Accept this fact, and face change
by designing innovative responses.

The Law of Dharma

Every individual is unique,
having different talents and needs.
Talents are to be expressed
and needs are to fulfilled
within the limits of Universal Dharma.

The Law of Karma

Everything in the phenomenal world
has a cause and a consequence.
Individuals create their destiny
by their moment-to-moment choices and actions.

The Law of Yajna

The existence of the world is
based upon the principle of Sacrifice –
mutual nourishing and cherishing,
or give and take.
Through sacrifice we receive;
in possessing we perish.

The Law of Yoga

The key to happiness is detachment,
the ability to impartially witness
our thoughts and actions amidst interaction.
Cherishing diverse perspectives
and solutions to issues of life is yoga.

The Law of Leela

Effective individuals expend the least energy
facing life's challenges and problems.
The relaxed and playful mind
gives maximum productivity or efficiency
and enjoys the experience of
self-exploration and self-expression.

These laws are distilled from
the entire Hindu Tradition
of seven thousand years.
By applying these laws in daily life,
one can unfold one's potentialities
and achieve maximum success.

Hari OM!
Swami Bodhananda Saraswati

Acknowledgements

The dedication of this book will not be complete without thanking those who helped me in its production.

Sri A.K.K. Nair, President Sambodh Foundation, Palakkad, organised my talks on 'Seven Hindu Spiritual Laws of Success' which from the basis of this book.

Dr. Sangeetha Menon, National Institute of Advanced Studies, Bangalore, prepared the first draft.

Dr. Ruth Harring, Trustee, The Sambodh Society, USA, edited the book.

Last, but not least, I am grateful to Srishti, particularly Jasjit Man Singh who gave this priority over her other work so it would be ready for my winter tour in Kerala.

This book was written especially keeping in mind youth who are in danger of losing touch with their moorings and for those who have had no exposure to the Indian traditions.

New Delhi
28 November 2003

Swami Bodhananda

Introduction

Our Hindu Tradition

The seven discourses presented in the following chapters are based upon the *Vedas*, the *Upanishads*, *Darshanas*, the *Bhagavad Gita* and the *Puranas* – the entire wisdom tradition of India covering a period of 7000 years. The Indian wisdom tradition has its roots in the *Vedas*. The *Upanishads*, which appear at the end of the *Vedas*, are its branches, the *Darshanas* are its flowers, and the *Bhagavad Gita* and the *Puranas* are the fruit. The *Seven Spiritual Laws*, presented here, are its nectar.

When I chose to call this book *The Seven Hindu Spiritual Laws of Success*, some people questioned, "Why use the word '*Hindu*?'" Or they suggest, "Why not title the book '*Vedic Spiritual Laws*,' or just '*Spiritual Laws*'?" These are very relevant questions, but allow me to explain.

I have consciously chosen the word '*Hindu*' as a part of this book's title. If I had used the term '*Vedic*,' those who encounter this book may misunderstand, thinking that what follows excludes the later *Upanishadic* and *Pauranic* developments that have taken place in India's spiritual and cultural history. In order to include *all* the later cultural development of India, I chose the word '*Hindu*.' This term was originally a Persian pronunciation of the word '*Sindhu*' – the name of the river along the banks of which Aryan *rishis* composed the Rig Vedic hymns. Thus, when we say '*Hindu*' we include the total historical experience of Indian culture up to contemporary times. In a distilled form, the title reflects this complex and profound experience.

Others have asked why I have used the word 'law' instead of '*tattva*' (principle) or 'metaphysics' or 'philosophy'? If I were to simply say '*tattva*,' it may suggest only an ideology. An ideology is someone's intellectual creation or product of an era. Ideologies come and go. An ideology is often merely an individual's subjective experience, frequently highly prejudiced and/or biased, and disappears with the demise of the individual who inspired it. Thus, to avoid that kind of confusion, I have consciously selected the word '*law*'. The word '*law*', being a much more precise term than the words '*tattva*', 'metaphysics' or 'principles', pertains to, or describes, the behavior of phenomena, events and objects. The term 'law' implies a statement of fact, the observable behavior of phenomenon.

The word *law* may be understood in a scientific sense – like *natural law*, a law concerning the behavior of natural phenomena, e.g. the Law of Gravity, a principle of physics which recognizes the attraction of smaller objects in space to larger objects. The scientist's statements should be true to the external event. The scientist engages in observing a phenomenon, searching for some pattern, either for the purpose of predicting those behaviors or for understanding or determining how a phenomenon behaves. Natural laws neither depend upon my likes or dislikes, nor your likes or dislikes. Natural laws do not depend upon the beliefs or preferences of a scientist. Furthermore, understanding a natural law helps. How so? When you understand any Law of Nature, you become capable of molding nature to your advantage.

In order to organize our lives for greater good and to achieve greater happiness, these seven Hindu Spiritual Laws are to be fully understood. For example, if you understand the behavior of an average human being, that awareness assists you in your relationships. How does an average human being structure his or her behavior? Man is a rational choice-maker, and psychologists have observed that every individual's behavior is primarily guided by concern for his or her own welfare. Understanding this psychological law, you can determine your behavior accordingly and, as a consequence, experience greater clarity, wellness and happiness in life.

Physical and Moral Corollaries

As citizens of a physical world, our understanding of the

physical Laws of Nature is vital to our well-being and happiness. We are affected by physical laws, by what happens in the physical world. If you know the Law of Gravity, you will not go up to the fourth floor of a building and jump out of a window. You understand that if you were to jump from that height, you would fall (according to Newton's Law of Gravity) at the rate of 36 feet per second, smashing your head on the ground. Understanding a law may contribute to the well-being of your life, that is, *if you apply that knowledge*! Similarly, an understanding of the ethical and moral laws that govern our relationships is very important to our ability to organize our behavior so as to attain greater happiness in life.

From experience, we have become aware of many physical laws. For example, by experience you understand that if you throw a ball against a wall, the ball bounces back to you. This is a simple law. Similarly, if you were to strike another person, he or she is likely to hit you back. This is our natural tendency. The moral law stated in the *Bhagavad Gita* translates: "Do unto others as you would have them do unto you" (6:32). Let's extrapolate from that law: how do you get another person to smile at you? You simply smile *at him*! When you smile, he smiles back. Likewise, when you hurt someone, he or she will hurt you in return. What goes around comes around. On the contrary, if, in the midst of a heated argument, someone strikes you and you do not hit back, we can surmise that you understand the higher moral law and have modified your behavior accordingly. Thus, by applying *this* law, *you* avoid being part of a mechanical cycle of conditioned response.

We understand, then, that there are moral and ethical laws that govern inter-personal relationships. Following such laws, life becomes a happy experience. Otherwise, life may become very miserable.

The Spiritual Laws

Essentially, we are spiritual beings, and our lives are grounded in Spirit, in Consciousness. Like the natural and moral laws that govern our universe, there are spiritual laws. Each chapter of this book will familiarize you with one of the seven spiritual laws and help you incorporate these laws into your everyday living.

The great Buddha says, "One law which is observable in human life is that all human beings are unhappy." You may agree or disagree, but this is a fact. Buddha observed human life, listened to others' stories, and experimented with his own life. Finally, he came to this great observation – "*Duhkham, duhkham, sarvatra*" – that the average human life is full of sorrow. But Buddha's insight did not end there. He went beyond and observed that suffering has a cause, and when you remove that cause, the effect also will be removed. The Buddha not only *said* that there is a way to escape from this suffering, but he *demonstrated* it as well. His Eight-fold Path encapsulates his experience and ideas.

Suffering is a trap that we walk into unsuspectingly – like our use of credit cards. Although, at first, we fail to realize it, the credit card is a source of great sorrow. When you are presented with a credit card, it comes along with pleasing words – "Just take it. It's free." But did you read the fine print? That same credit card, which you thought promised freedom, is capable of taking you into a debt-trap out of which you will rarely escape! The credit card industry presents a new form of "colonization" of the human mind. By using a credit card, you actually lend *yourself* into the vicious hands of moneylenders. You are helping *them*, rather than their helping you! Now your problem is compounded, your freedom restricted by the burden of debt, and your happiness displaced by suffering.

Spiritual Sadhana – Putting Laws into Practice

In the coming chapters, I have distilled the seven spiritual laws from the collective experience of our Indian wisdom tradition. During the course of reading this book, you will be discovering the spiritual laws that the *rishis* first enunciated and practiced in their material and social life. By following them they were freed from the snare of sorrow. Like the ancient *rishis*, with this awareness, we too can become capable of applying the seven spiritual laws and of living in accordance with this wisdom. As a result we, too, can enjoy the spontaneous happiness achieved by the *rishis* of yore. That is the ultimate purpose of these laws and the reason behind this book – to help the reader "organize" his or her life for happiness *and* freedom. Unfortunately, we rarely give much attention to *spiritual* laws, and our suffering increases. In spite of our awareness of all kinds of laws – political, economic, and scientific – people are still unhappy! Despite all our material knowledge, why are we unable to enhance the essential quality of our lives?

When we achieve understanding of these laws that govern our world of interactions and experience, we escape the trap of sorrow and misery into which we have fallen. But mere understanding of a law is not enough. We must actively apply that law in our daily life and derive the benefit from our understanding. The application of a spiritual law in our lives is what we call '*sadhana*'. First, know. Then practice and make life a rich experience.

Seven Hindu Spiritual Laws – an Overview

The seven Spiritual Laws begin with the all-encompassing *Law of Brahman* and are successive in their application. The first two laws are more subtle, cosmic laws. The third law, the *Law of Dharma*, provides a linkage between the cosmic and subjective domains. The next three laws – *Karma*, *Yajna* and *Yoga* – apply more directly to the subject – the individual consciousness. The final law, the *Law of Leela*, is the summation of all the previous laws, and its application depends upon one's successfully understanding and implementing all these previous laws.

Three Cosmic Laws

1. The first spiritual law of life is the ***Law of Brahman***. *Brahman* is a word that you may know or recognize from your reading of *Vedanta*. But we mistakenly think that *Brahman* – Absolute Reality or Consciousness – is to be meditated upon by people who have retired from life and have moved to some remote place for life's final spiritual fulfillment. This book will reverse your thinking and demonstrate that the *Law of Brahman* is very applicable *in the very midst* of your practical life!

The *Law of Brahman* states that existence is a Field of Infinite Potentialities and is grounded in Consciousness. The *Aitreya Upanishad* of the *Rig Veda* declares, "*Prajnanam brahmaa.*" "Consciousness is *Brahman*" (3:3). One *Upanishadic mahavakya* (a statement of profound wisdom) takes that notion one step further, asserting "*Tattvamasi,*" "That Thou Art!" (*Chandogya Upanishad* 6:8.7). Hence, our Hindu wisdom tradition not only understands *Brahman* as the All-Pervading Consciousness, the ground of existence, but it simultaneously declares that *you* are that existence and expression of *Brahman*.

You *are* that *Field of Infinite Potentialities.*

The question is how do we understand and apply this law? How do we make sense out of this declaration that, "I am *Brahman*; I am Infinite Potentiality?" while living in a complex culture and era? How do we formulate a program of *sadhana* based upon that law? The *Law of Brahman*, which is the distillation of the *Upanishadic mahavakyas*, requires further definition, exploration and meditation. This you will find in Chapter 1, "*The Spiritual Law of Brahman.*"

2. The ***Law of Maya*** follows naturally from our understanding of the *Law of Brahman* and is of equal importance. That word '*maya*' may be familiar to you, but until now, *maya* has probably been just a metaphysical concept. We may have even heard our parents or friends and associates exclaim, "It's all *maya*," implying "It is an illusion." We may have even made this remark ourselves. If you fail in an examination or lose an important tennis match, your defensive mechanism is, "After all, what does it matter? It's only *maya*." With this thought in mind, you sit back complacently thinking that you have solved the problem. But adopting such an attitude doesn't help you in understanding and organizing your life. *Maya* describes the Law of Change and the need for quiet, creative responses to unpredictable situations. Understand the *Law of Maya*, apply it and grow – a simple formula for success.

3. The third law is the ***Law of Dharma***. *Dharma* is another word that we hear frequently. In India we also discuss

refinements or extensions of this term – *Sanatana Dharma* (Eternal Laws), *varnashrama dharma* (socio-cultural laws) and *svadharma* (subjective laws). These are all applications of the word '*dharma*' in various contexts, but often we do not understand the deeper implications of *Law of Dharma*.

Every individual has his or her unique *dharma*, which manifests in a particular situation. To activate our inner powers, we must recognize and organize our lives according to our *dharma* and, from that unique vantage point, combining inner discipline with the dynamic outer environment, design our responses to this ever-changing world. The meaning of *dharma* along with these issues will be presented in Chapter 3. By applying the *Law of Dharma* in our daily life, we will attain spiritual freedom, unconditioned happiness, while living in this world – what we call '*moksa*.'

Three Subjective Laws

4. When you come to the subjective domain of individual mind and thought, there is another set of universal laws. The first of these is the ***Law of Karma***. The *Law of Karma* states every individual is an independent center of initiative, i.e. you are responsible for your destiny. The *Law of Karma* affirms that the Supreme Truth, *Brahman*, expresses through you *as your choices*. Thought by thought, deed by deed, you create your self. Whether or not we use this ability, we each have that

freedom. These things we will discuss further and try to understand in Chapter 4. In the process, you will – for the first time – experience *real* freedom!

5. The fifth law is the ***Law of Yajna***. The word, *yajna*, means 'sacrifice,' so we may alternately say, the *Law of Sacrifice*. We find the *yajna* principle basic to the operation of the natural, phenomenal world supporting human relationships. Someone or something sacrifices for someone or something else. It is the law of mutually nourishing and cherishing, creating win-win situations. Refusing to follow or disobeying this law invites misery and sorrow. Chapter 5 focuses on understanding the dynamics and centrality of *yajna* to the micro- and macrocosmic dimensions of existence.

6. Next, is the ***Law of Yoga***. The word *yoga* comes from the root '*yuj*,' which means 'to unite' or 'to yoke' with the Self or with God. In the *Bhagavad Gita* the word *yoga*, ironically, is given the opposite meaning – 'detachment,' or to *disunite* with your suffering, or stated another way, 'to dissociate with your association with suffering.' If you can distill all ancient Eastern spiritual wisdom into one word, it is 'detachment.' The message of the *Bhagavad Gita* is *tyagam*, detachment. That is also what Ramakrishna advocated, '*tyagam,*' to detach. Detachment is the final accomplishment, the final *yoga*.

By detachment we mean the process and the power of dissociating with suffering and, therefore, uniting with the Self. By following the *Law of Yoga*, you acquire the inner leisure to listen to the voice of the soul and enable yourself to keep your mind in balance amidst life's complex situations. In the process of Self-actualization, skillfully applying the tool of detachment, you automatically choose the right responses. Such a person – one who is detached *and* engaged – is called a *yogi*. We will learn more about this possibility and its application in Chapter 6.

Leela – the Summation of Spiritual Laws

7. The last of our seven spiritual laws is the ***Law of Leela***. *Leela* means 'effortlessness,' 'playfulness.' If you are playful (in the spiritual sense of that word) having a deep understanding of your true nature, you can be more effective, more successful, and will have better relationships. Most of us are serious and anxious all the time, with long faces and several lines on our foreheads – looking as though we are responsible for running the whole world! As a result, you invite all kinds of illnesses and attract failure. But if one understands the *leelanyaya* – the *Law of Playfulness,* that person becomes 'playful.' Chapter 7 helps us to learning to apply this law, moment to moment, in our everyday lives; we can remain 'cool' amidst the most strenuous pursuits and daily activities. Then life will unfold as a series of blissful experiences.

These, then, are the seven spiritual laws that we will explore in this book – *Brahman, Maya, Dharma, Karma, Yajna, Yoga,*

Leela – following which, you will move from a life of *samsara* or misery and sorrow to the life of *moksa, sayujya, nirvana* or liberation.

To the best of my ability I place this knowledge before you for your consideration, for your reflection. Now it is for you to read and reflect upon and, finally, to put all this into practice so that you can move from your present life of *samsara,* or suffering, into the dream-life of *nirvana*, *moksa*, spiritual freedom. Ultimately, freedom is that ability to make use of your environment to explore your potential and to express that Infinite Potential *while* interacting with the world. This is the meaning of *moksa.*

One

The Spiritual Law of Brahman

Your Divine Human Potential

The *Law of Brahman* says, "Existence is a Field of Infinite Potentialities." This statement is not to entertain or intoxicate you. It is not a story, but a statement of fact. If understood properly, this statement will bring great clarity to your life and aspirations: "Existence is a field of Infinite Potentialities." Pay close attention to its meaning, especially if you want to achieve something great in life – to become a better citizen, a better parent, a better housewife, politician, lawyer, manager, worker – a better person in any walk of life.

These laws are meant for very active people, for people who want to achieve greater success, to explore and unfold their *full* human potential, to go to the very depth of life and the very height of existence. These laws are for adventurous people, not for people whose primary aspirations are to merely sleep, eat, grow old and die! These laws are for people who strive to be very active and dynamic, who want to create a niche for themselves in this world so that they leave a better world than what they found when they entered. That should be the spirit in which the *Law of Brahman* is understood and applied!

The question is: How do we understand this statement – "Existence is a Field of Infinite Potentialities?" Our more immediate concern is apt to be about making meaning out of our complex lives and much less about understanding the philosophical notion, "I am *Brahman*; I am Infinite Potential." If this is the case, I have news for you. Making sense out of life will ultimately *lead* you to this question and, hence, to the *Law of Brahman* governing life itself. This chapter is designed to help you understand this law and its ramifications so that you *can* apply it in your everyday world.

The Self-Conscious, Self-Evident Self of All

Let us begin by examining the meaning of the Sanskrit word, *Brahman,* what this word refers to and what it seeks to encapsulate. The word *Brahman* is derived from the root, *brh*, which means, literally, "That which is big," thus, Brahman means "*brihatvat brahma*" – "the All-Accommodating." The word *Brahman* indicates Reality rather than explaining it. It refers to "That which cannot be described," except obliquely by using references derived from the familiar. The problem is one of describing the Indescribable, as *Brahman* cannot be realized through the senses or by logic. *Brahman* – the all-encompassing, all-pervading, inexhaustible, indivisible, pure source and support of all – is discerned by the subtle mind, as the *Taittiriya Upanishad* tells us, in the "cave of the heart."

Our individual body-mind mediates between Consciousness, or the Self, and the world. We are aware of the world around us. Furthermore, we are aware that we are aware. If you doubt your existence, I only have to ask, "Are you conscious of that doubt?" The answer is obvious – "Yes, I am conscious of that doubt." My next question is, "Who is aware of that doubt?" You may fall silent, or you may again say, "*I* am conscious." Then, allow me to ask, "Who is that 'I'?"

That 'I' is consciousness itself! Consciousness is self-evident. Finally, you have to admit, "I am That!" This realization is an awakening for you.

That you exist or that I exist is a self-evident fact, a self-evident experience. You cannot deny your existence, nor can I deny my existence. Existence is a primary experience. You may doubt your existence, but that doubt itself is proof of your existence! To doubt is to exist. Then what is existence? We may agree that a particular object exists, for example, a chair. But tomorrow the chair may not be there, so what exactly is existence? Existence challenges our understanding and defies explanation.

That Field of Infinite Potentiality That You Are

Let me point out the Law of Existence. The law says that

existence is a field – a *Field of Infinite Potentialities*. That is the law, and that law also says, "That *Field of Infinite Potentialities* is not different from you, not other than you, the '*experiencer*' of existence." This law has two facets. The first is that existence – which is self-evident – is a field of Infinite Potentialities, and, secondly, *you are* that existence, *you are a Field of Infinite Potentialities*! You may not be able to *see* this fact, just as you are unable to *see* the Law of Gravity, or take its picture or put gravity in a test tube. Gravity doesn't require your *belief* to exist or function. However, if you want to experience the Law of Gravity, as proof of its existence, just climb up a tall coconut tree and, when you reach the top, let go. Then you will understand! Experience will teach you the lesson of gravity! Gravity may be an invisible force, but when you fall you will have proven to yourself that it exists!

Similarly, when the *Upanishads* proclaim that you are a Field of Infinite Potentialities, you may not *see* it, but if you meditate upon it and act according to this Law you *realize* it. Your feelings, your thoughts and your actions become channels of experiencing your Infinite Potentiality. For those who need proof, experience is the only method. Gravity is an operational law that we understand inferentially by witnessing its effects in the material world.

A similar problem of proof arises in our *belief* that we are a field of unlimited potentiality. Believing this does not solve our problem. We need to test this statement.

The law further states that this Field of Infinite Potentialities is *subjective*; you can never objectify *Brahman*. That means *you* – the subjective consciousness – are the Field of Infinite Potentiality. Such a statement cannot be ascertained through the operations of the sense organs.

Processing the Law of your Potentiality

In order to understand that you are that Field of Infinite Potentialities, you have to take up meditation and process this law in the silence of your heart. In that space, you may realize your true identity. From that understanding various disciplines can be devised. How are we to utilize that information? And what kind of thought process is necessary to actualize this understanding? Those details we will discuss later. Meanwhile, this law is to be ingrained in your thinking – that "I am that Field of Infinite Potentiality."

Stated another way, *Brahman* is your subjectivity, your Real nature. Your Real nature is this non-objective reality, *Brahman*. Allow me to explain. You cannot *see* your true nature as an object. You *experience Brahman* as a subject. This subjective reality – the Field of Infinite Potentialities – is *in*visible and *in*divisible. *Brahman* cannot be seen, although you may travel all over the world with a microscope or a telescope searching for *Brahman*. *That Brahman is the nature of the seer*, your subjectivity, your consciousness. The fact that you are that Field of Infinite Potentiality means that you cannot *see Brahman* as an object outside, because it is your subjectivity, your consciousness.

Furthermore, this Field of Infinite Potentialities cannot be further dissolved or divided. It is an indivisible field. You cannot further reduce it into component units, like the atom which can be further split into the proton, electron and neutron. But take the example of space – can you cut space into small pieces? You cannot. Similarly, the Field of Infinite Potentiality is such that we cannot further dismantle or dismember it, or deconstruct it. Nowadays, there are philosophers who try to deconstruct everything into nothingness. But their pursuit becomes futile when applied to this Field of Infinite Potentialities. No philosopher can deconstruct the indivisible *Brahman*.

Indivisibility also means inexhaustibility. Like space, *Brahman* is an Inexhaustible Field of Potentiality: The *Bhagavad Gita* says, "*Bijam mam sarva-bhutanam viddhi Partha sanatanam...*" that *Brahman* is "the eternal seed of endless manifestation" (7:10). Stated another way, *Brahman* is Infinite Intelligence. Likewise, *you* are that Infinite Intelligence, that Infinite Power, that Field of Infinite Potential. That is the law, which – for your own well-being – you ought to understand and act accordingly to remove your suffering and misery. The fact of your true nature is a law, just like the Law of Gravity. It is better to realize that fact and apply that understanding in your life. That is, modify your behavior according to your understanding – that you are that Immortal Spirit.

This indivisible, invisible, subjective Field of Infinite Potentialities is also called Spirit – *not* that sort of spirit which you imbibe in the evening! That may also give you some inspiration, making you very enthusiastic and energetic. But its effect lasts only a few hours and then it wears off. We are discussing a deeper, all-encompassing field of experience. "This indivisible, invisible, subjective Field of Potentialities is that which I am." That you are! Repeat that statement out loud, then mentally, breathe it in and out; meditate upon it. This truth is to be understood.

Expressing Infinite Energy

When you have understood the fact of your True Nature, then you also come to understand that this Infinite Potentiality is always "anxious" to express. That is another beauty of *Brahman* – it is so full, it is always ready and eager to express. There is infinite energy – a need for this Spirit to express.

The energy of *Brahman* may be explained something like this: When you are full of music and you have a large repertoire, it hums inside your head. Then, one day, you find a few people seated in front of you. Won't you have an urge to sing? If there is an opportunity – a ripe condition – and inside you are *filled* with music, an urge to express will naturally follow. If you have no knowledge of or talent for music and an opportunity descends upon you, the occasion becomes a calamity. You panic, "What will I do? How do I get out of this predicament?" But, if you have talent and the conditions arise, then your ability will manifest.

Brahman has an inherent urge to express its potentiality. That is a *Law of Brahman*. That is why in the *Upanishad* it is said, "*So'kamayata; Bahu syam prajayeyeti*" – "The Universal Self, *Brahman*, desired, 'May I become many.' Then He practiced austerities, conscious of that thought; He manifested the entire universe of beings and objects and then entered into them. Having entered into them, He became gross and subtle form; determinate and indeterminate entities; the substratum and the substrated; knowledge and ignorance. This Truth became the Real as well as the unreal" (*Taittiriya Upanishad*. 2:6).

This Reality, this Infinite Potentiality, has a compelling desire to spread its wings, to display, to flower forth, to dance its joy and glory – behold a dancing *Brahman*! Not just a cold, stony, lifeless *Brahman*, melancholy and depressed, cringing in some confined corner. The *Upanishad* says that *Brahman* has an *urge* to express, and that expressive urge each one of us has, because *Brahman is our true nature.*

At times, all of us have experienced that urge. We've all complained, at one time or another, "Nobody lets me be myself; no one allows me to express myself." You want an opportunity. When you do not express, you feel suppressed. When you are suppressed, you become manipulative and crooked. You even sit crookedly, like a question mark, and ask useless, pointless questions: "Swamiji, why did the Lord create the world? Why is this life so full of suffering? When will my miseries end? When will the Lord lift me from this mortal life?" These types of questions are asked because we are not expressing; we are not growing; we are not learning; we are not expanding; we are not exploring our unlimited potential.

When we understand this law – that I am a Field of Infinite Potentiality – and when conditions are fulfilled, we *must* express. If there are no conditions, then one has to create a condition and then express. If you don't create that condition and express, then unhappiness and dissatisfaction will be your lot in life. Dissatisfaction results when you are obstructed or hindered in your self-expression.

Most of us are dissatisfied people because this profound realization is lacking, that "I am that Infinite Potential." Think it. Feel it. Breathe it. Say it: "I am that Field of Infinite Potentiality!" Believe it. Accept it. This law is found everywhere in the world, in all disciplines – in science, in human interaction, in all fields of endeavor and relationship.

Quantum Corollaries

For example, in their own jargon, physicists talk about "the quantum field of infinite possibilities." The physicists have broken down everything into atoms and finally into quantum fields. The "quantum field" is another way of saying the "Field of Infinite Potentialities." The quantum field – a spectrum of possibilities – can express as a quanta or as a wave and form the raw material for the created universe.

Let me provide another example. Biologists also talk about the infinite potentialities of a cell. You first existed as a cell clinging to the wall of your mother's womb – a single, tiny cell, 46 chromosomes composed of 23 chromosomes from your mother, 23 from you father – a unicellular speck. Such a cell has infinite potentialities. It can divide itself into further cells. These first 135 cells are called stem cells. Stem cells can become brain cells, bone cells, skin cells, heart cells, blood cells – potentially performing any function. Although stem cells have infinite potentialities, over a period of time they specialize and forget their versatility, just as when you specialize in one field, your other talents remain dormant as you manifest your specialization. After some time you forget that, too, and then you age and die. So, also your cells specialize, age, cease to function, and, over a period of time, disintegrate.

Now scientists discuss cloning. One cell is taken, activated by means of certain chemical processes, allowing it to remember its entire potentiality, and then another creature is created from that single, original cell. Whether you follow the path of biology or physics, or spirituality, you will eventually come to understand that there is infinite potential latent in each one of us.

Each of us is a Field, and we have a need to express our Infinite Potentiality. Generally, that expression takes place through the medium of desire-fulfilling projects. As we learned from the *Taittiriya Upanishad*, "*So'kamayata*," "*Brahman desires*" to express its potential power, meaning, the very ground of our existence is that innate creative urge.

Desire as Creative Expression

Once, in Palakkad, Kerala, I had the unexpected pleasure of visiting a very unusual garden made entirely from cotton thread. This "thread garden" is situated near the Madura Coats Thread factory. From strands of rejected thread, an ingenious artist created a world of exquisite beauty – plants, flowers, leaves and fruit. If one were to dismantle all of the artist's creations only bundles of thread would be left. By themselves, these bundles of thread offer no essential meaning or inspiration. However, fueled by a desire to create and inspired by his ideas, an imaginative person created a magnificent garden from mere bundles of discarded thread. These few bundles of thread would have little meaning for most of us; we would just kick them around or throw them away. But, for a person with artistic sensibilities, this multitude of splendidly colored threads became a medium to express imaginative powers. You and I could not imagine such a thing, but the artist saw the potential in these insignificant bundles of ordinary thread, and, using his imagination, created this wonderful, panoramic world of beauty.

Similarly, while a stone remains meaningless for us, a sculptor may pick it up and carve a magnificent statue. We ourselves may think of sitting on that stone or of carving our initials into it. That is the maximum we would do, whereas another person overflowing with ideas sees many possibilities in that stone. Using his chisel and hammer, little by little, he chips off a few corners, and, over a period of several days, a beautiful idol of Lord Krishna appears. Neither you nor I saw Krishna in that black stone; but the sculptor saw Him. He could visualize the image and invoke a possibility latent in that stone that no one else could see!

That creative possibility is, likewise, hidden in that bundle of thread, or in a lump of clay, in a bar of gold, or in ordinary stone – or in you! Creativity is always latent, lying unexpressed – but you must have vision to see possibilities and the urge to create. When that creative urge arises, fired by imagination, one can create any variety of things: that is freedom and becomes one's unique expression.

From the invisible, raw material, which we called the *Field of Potentialities*, we may express our creativity. And where is that Field of Potentialities? In the *Bhagavad Gita*, Krishna says, "That *Field of Infinite Potentialities* is identical to *your* subjective consciousness. Of course, an artist may have to obtain some essential materials or objects. But where does one find the raw material for true creativity, true freedom? Where do we find that infinite potentiality? According to the *Upanishads*, it is found in our subjective consciousness. Now we ask, "Where is the locus of subjective consciousness?"

The Subjective Consciousness

You don't have to go in search of that subjective consciousness. Consciousness is your *pratyagatma* – your "innermost subjectivity." By closing our eyes, keeping our minds quiet, we access that consciousness. Your subjective consciousness is the window to this *Field of Pure Potentiality.* By creating a contemplative mode of mind, you are establishing access – connectivity – connecting to that Field. Hence, the *rishi* asserts, "*Tat tvam asi*" – "Thou art That!" That *Field of Infinite Potentiality*, that creative possibility, is identical to your subjective consciousness.

When the *rishi* says, "*Tat tvam asi*" – "That you are" – don't look around the room to see what object he is referring to! Once in an *ashram* it so happened that a *guru* said to his *sisya*, a young student, "*Tat tvam asi*," and the boy looked around. Seeing a donkey passing by, the boy thought the *guru* was implying, "You are that; you are an ass!" And, feeling very insulted, he left that *ashram*, permanently. Of course, the *rishis* never intended that particular meaning, but that is the way an extroverted mind would understand the meaning of *Tat tvam asi.*

Tat tvam asi means, "Consciousness is your essential nature." Consciousness is subjective; Consciousness is invisible until (and unless) you express it! Similarly, where were all the flowers in the thread garden? One could see them only once the artist expressed his creativity, gave form and life to the garden. When we give expression to our ideas, then alone does this invisible subjective *Field of Potentialities* manifest.

When you express – even though you never thought about it previously – you may realize, "Consciousness is already there!" The *Field of Infinite Potentiality* is subjective; it *is* Consciousness; it is invisible and indivisible. Since it is indivisible, it is inexhaustible. The *Law of Brahman* suggests all this.

To summarize: *Brahman* is an inexhaustible *Field of Infinite Possibilities and Potentialities*, and that *Brahman* is the unmanifest, subjective self. That invisible, indivisible, subjective self, which is the Field, requires expression. That expression is achieved through the medium of desire. Your desire-fulfilling activities are the technology – the means of your achieving self-expression.

Four Goals of Life

In Indian culture we have identified four legitimate goals for humankind. The first goal is *dharma*, then *artha*, then *kama*, and then *moksa.* (Translated into English, these Sanskrit terms mean: a) ethical means or righteousness; b) wealth or comfort;

c) pleasure; and, d) liberation.) *Artha* and *kama* are material, visible goals. Your pursuit of *artha* and *kama* is to be tempered or restrained by consideration of *dharma*. The consideration of *dharma* is vital. What exactly is *dharma*? *Dharma* means "that which holds together" – implying ethical and moral values or social mores which support both social and cultural life and are instrumental in attaining life's highest goal – *moksa*.

Within the parameters of *dharma*, you can pursue these two goals – *artha* and *kama*. If these goals are pursued within the parameters of *dharma*, then you will not inflict any damage upon the environment. Nor will you cause any damage in your social relationships or to your individual health. The health of the individual, the family, the society, and the environment will be maintained if you pursue these goals – *artha* and *kama* (wealth and pleasures or comfort) within the boundaries set by *dharma*.

Comfort gives you immediate gratification, and wealth gives you long term security. When you eat your breakfast, you feel satisfaction. Only after eating do your worries begin – "Will there be any lunch for me today?" Survival is a natural worry. Food is a human survival need. You must ensure your lunch, your dinner – in essence, your survival. For an intelligent human being, who can anticipate the future, the need for security arises. All of us understand the need for security.

The scriptures say that you may pursue these legitimate human needs and goals, but within the limits of *dharma*. As you pursue the goals of *kama* and *artha* with the awareness that *Brahman* is your true nature, you actualize yourself, manifesting the Spirit in the midst of activity. That is the meaning of freedom. Freedom means manifesting that inner spirit continuously as you are pursuing your material goals. Unless this is understood, one fails to realize the necessity of desire. Desire is the fuel for self-actualization!

The Truth of Desire Projects

Desires are two types. One desire is to grab and to possess. The other desire is to create and to share. The person who created the thread garden had a desire to create and share. He trained people, procured the raw material, had an idea and felt the urge to express it. After expressing, he did not just selfishly sit and admire his work, enjoying the garden all by himself. He threw the gates wide open and invited everyone inside. Anyone who wants to come and enjoy the thread garden can wander and marvel at the results of this person's creative effort, experience that transcendence inherent to the artist's expression. Overflowing creativity and a desire to share, the artist created the garden for self-expression.

Wherever there is a creative experience, there is a sharing experience. When you are not creative, you want to grab, to hold and possess, and to deny others the joy of sharing. That is called *self-centered* desire. The thread garden is an example of *self-giving* desire. The more you expand the amplitude of your desire – sharing abundantly – the more you unfold your creative potential in self-expression. To the extent that your amplitude reduces and contracts during the course of your pursuing and fulfilling desires, you become suppressed.

Desire is to be properly understood. Desire ought to be an all-embracing desire, a desire to share and not a smothering desire, a desire to possess. By pursuing legitimate needs and goals – our desires – within the limits of *dharma*, we can interact with the world and simultaneously unfold our unique potential.

Applying the Law of Brahman

The *Law of Brahman* and its various dimensions and depths are to be explored and made part of your behavior. If the law is not part of your behavior, then, for you *Brahman* has no meaning at all. Just as an adult no longer behaves as the child who innocently reaches out to touch a flame, for one who understands, this law becomes part of the behavior. One should no longer think, feel or behave like an isolated field of *limited* potentiality. Having understood the Law of Gravity and its consequences being part of our experience, we don't jump off of high buildings. Application is the only method by which we can make meaning out of these laws. Otherwise these laws are just bits of verbal information floating inside our brains.

Knowledge unapplied is a mere burden!

How do you apply the *Law of Brahman*? First, believe in that law and act in accordance. For example, there is a physical law specifying that when you heat water to 100 degrees centigrade it will evaporate and become vapor. Now you ask, "How do I know that if I heat the water to that temperature it will vaporize?" You only know when you apply that law and observe for sometime. When you apply that law and are patient, you see how the law operates. If the water does not vaporize, then you either wait patiently or explore and try to find the reason – for example, it may be the altitude affecting the boiling point of the water.

First of all, have the faith, and then – based upon that faith – act according to the *Law of Brahman* – meditating upon your *fullness* something like this: "I am infinite. I am not a limited, miserable worm. My infinitude may presently be invisible to me. Nor is my infinitude visible to another. What is apparent to me is my finitude. What is apparent to others about me is my finitude, my wretched nature. Both of us are unconscious of our infinitude. But when I express, my infinitude manifests. What is invisible is made into the visible, into phenomena, into something that can be experienced by me and by others." One has to believe very ardently and reflect upon this.

Krishna says in the *Bhagavad Gita*, "*Na tvevaham jatu nasam na tvam n'eme jan'adhipah / nac'aiva na bhavisyamah sarve vayam atah param.*" "There was never a time when I did not exist, nor you…nor shall all of us cease to be hereafter" (2:12). The verse posits, "We all are that *Infinite Field*, and that *Infinite Field* is our nature." "You are an *Infinite Field.* I am an *Infinite Field,*" Krishna declares. Even Duryodhana, who cheated the *Pandavas* at a game of dice, is that *Infinite Field of Potentiality*. The poor man – he did not know; therefore, he failed to apply that law, became crooked and created misery for himself and others!

When you chant this *mantra*, "*Shivoham,*" what does that mean? It means, "You *are* that Infinite Field" – it doesn't mean that you dress up like *Shiva* with two snakes slithering around your neck, with matted hair adorned with an artificial crescent moon balancing on your head, and in that costume go dancing in the nearby burial ground! Even ghosts will run away from you! That is not the idea. The idea is to understand your self as this Infinite Power; and further, that through contemplative consciousness we can live in constant touch with that Infinite Power. Through appropriate feelings, thoughts and actions, you come to actualize your potential. This is how we are to understand and apply the first law – the *Law of Brahman.*

People sometimes remark, "Swamiji, *I might* take myself as Infinite, but what about others who may not accept that I am." Need for approval from others is an expression of your weakness and veils your blessedness. It is not for others' sake that you are trying to become established in who you are! You are only exercising your birthright! On their own, others will slowly recognize this law. Even if they don't recognize your infinitude, why should it matter to you? Others are not the problem! You are the problem! Your self-imposed limitation is the problem. Throw away that thought-created limitation. Apply the *Law of Brahman*, and in the process, even if you die, you will die a hero's death. Stretch to the limits of your potential! How vast is your potential!

The Challenge of Application

If we were to see a steep mountain, like a cathedral rising up in the distance, tell me, how many youngsters wouldn't aspire to climb that rock? A mountain represents a challenge, a means for us to explore our potential. But, instead of taking up that challenge, we adults recoil, "No, no. If I climb up there, I may fall down and die." Then you had better die – because there is little point in living like a worm. Here is a challenge, an invitation to climb the mountain! It is an opportunity for you to explore who you are. And we dare not face that challenge!

If you were to die in that effort of climbing, a thousand youngsters will rise up and, walking in your footsteps, face the same challenge. Slowly mankind will master the art of climbing that mountain. Your death will represent a possibility; it will serve as an inspiration for others to surpass you. But how many of us think in these terms? How many of us seek to transcend our petty limitations, to realize our goals, our potential? Instead we recoil in fear, "How can I possibly do that? I may break my leg and be permanently disabled." We accept ourselves as limited and reject a challenge!

Nature is constantly challenging us: "Come, wrestle with me; engage me and discover your potential!" And yet we feel no challenge! Patanjali says, "*Prakasa-kriya-sthiti silam bhutendriyatmakam / bhogaparvargartham drsyam.*" "This *prakriti* (the objective world of the senses and sense objects) is an aggregate of three energies – the energy of illumination, activity and inertia (*prakasa*, *kriya* and *sthiti*). The universe exists in order that the *experiencer* may enjoy it and, thus, become liberated" (*Yoga Sutras.* 2:18). This *prakriti* – physical and mental – is for your enjoyment. *Prakriti* will challenge you; she will tease and inspire you, and if you respond, life will be a very enthralling experience.

But people think, "It is not within me to take a risk, to respond to the creative urge, nor to succeed." Nor will parents allow their children to take risks. Instead they say consolingly, "Son, don't take any risks. Stay home. Your friends may go, but not you. You stay here." Instead, we must encourage our children to take risks! As the wise have said, "The only risk in life is not taking any risk!" Not taking any risk *is* the greatest risk – *and* the greatest loss.

Exploring Your Infinite Potential

By engaging in the outer challenges we are able to go deeply into ourselves and explore our unique potential, not by sitting somewhere and sleeping in the name of meditation. Most of the time when you close your eyes to meditate nothing happens and you fall asleep! Engagement is vital to your spiritual unfoldment – a healthful, happy, fulfilled life.

Applying this law, you will be able to understand your nature and actualize that nature in millions of varieties of ways. Through that Self-expression, total fulfillment, freedom, *moksa* is possible *while living in this world*. For that, the other six laws in the coming chapters will help you – the *Law of Maya*, the *Law of Dharma*, the *Laws of Karma*, *Yajna*, *Yoga* and *Leela*. But first you must try to put the *Law of Brahman* into practice.

Begin by accepting, "I am that Infinite," and dream big. Think big, and desire to express yourself. Then you will see *kundalini*, your coiled-up, suppressed energy arise, spreading its 1000 hoods – as Krishna says, "*Divi surya-saharasya*" – "like a thousand suns simultaneously arising" (*Gita*. 9:12). And through those 1000 hoods, your *Infinite Potentiality* will unfold!

These four things are to be understood from this Chapter on the *Law of Brahman* – what was elaborated upon as the subjective self, that Field of Infinite Potentiality: 1) that *Brahman* is invisible and requires expression which is achieved through desire-fulfilling projects; 2) that desire should be an encompassing desire to share, to bring out your *Self*; 3) desire often involves taking up a challenge or a risk to discover your potential, and: 4) the *Law of Brahman* is not only to be known, but is to be realized in application, by trial and error, experimentation and success. Applying the *Law of Brahman* is the *beginning* of your spiritual redemption. It is the beginning of your Self-unfoldment.

Two

The Spiritual Law of Maya

Change and the Spirit of Flow

The second law, The *Law of Maya*, says that the entire phenomenal world is constantly changing. By the phenomenal world we mean the manifest world that we see and experience. That world around and within you is the object of your experience. And this entire world experienced by you, the subjective consciousness, is an ever-changing flow. Change is inevitable, an ironclad Law of Nature. If we try to stop change we come under Nature's heavy boot. Instead of "going with the flow," we try to interrupt change and resist the *Law of Maya* and, in the process, become the victim of change.

Change is Nature's Law. Still, we attempt to *change* change! Why do we resist change? The tangible and visible evidence of our resistance is that none of us want to become old. When I ask a middle-aged person, "How old are you?" his or her reply generally is something like, "Oh, a little over thirty-five." We don't want to admit how old we really are because we are all trying to resist change – first by our words, then by our pretensions, and finally by plastic surgery! By electing to undergo plastic surgery we are only trying to look young again.

Instead of using the Law of Change for our own fulfillment, instead of flowing with it, we try to defy that law by various stratagems, we finally end up looking funny. Through plastic surgery one loses proportion, in short, a monster. Plastic surgery doesn't add to one's beauty. Your face might be that of a 16 year-old, but everywhere else you are very much seventy. What an incongruous look! Seventy trying to look like sixteen! Your appearance is without any proportion or measure, a whitewash of the natural process of aging. I am not talking about a young person who gets facial surgery to remove scars. Because we resist the law, that everything must change, we become its victim. Let us be reasonable – if things must change, then why try to stop this process?

The *Law of Maya* says that this constant flux and flow is the "tool" of *Brahman*. If we can't stem the tide of change, then we had better use our innate intelligence and learn to "ride" on change, that is, to apply that *Law of Change*, the *Law of Maya*. If we observe and apply that law, then our understanding of life will be greater and the changes that we experience will be easier. One must accept change, flow with change, but more importantly, *use change* as a way of unfolding, exploring and expressing oneself. To be in step with Nature, be ready to change, keep moving. Initiate change, and you will be one step ahead of Nature. Be ever-ready to change, innovate, and respond positively – not from our past conditionings, but from the *Spirit*.

Adi Sankaracharya's Definition of Maya

Now, let us try to understand that law which is enshrined in the Theory of *Maya*. There are various definitions of *maya*. In *Tattva Bodha*, Adi Sankaracharya says, "*Brahmashraya sattva rajas tamogunatmika maya asti*" (7). *Tattva Bodha* tells us that *maya* is "*trigunatmika*" – "made up of three energies" (the three *gunas*: *sattva*, *rajas* and *tamas*) and that these three energies are dependent upon *Brahman* – they are another "tool" of *Brahman*. *Brahman* uses *maya* as a tool to express itself. It is something like a musician, for example, Ravi Shankar, who takes a sitar having multiple strings, plays the instrument and in the process expresses himself. For Ravi Shankar, the sitar presents an opportunity. This is because he has confidence, because he applies that *first* law which declares, "You are that *Field of Infinite Potentiality*!"

To use this *Law of Change* or *Maya*, we need to understand *maya's* three energies – *sattva*, *rajas* and *tamas*. The tools of *Brahman* are also *our* tools! *Sattva* is a certain energy by which we cognize things. *Rajas* is an energy by which we act and move from place to place – the *Law of Motion*. Finally, *tamas* is an energy by which everything is stabilized. These energies operate as a dynamic, interactive balance.

Understanding the Dynamic Triguna

The three *gunas* or qualities that comprise *maya's* make-up are illuminating intellect, active engagement, and inertia or a restraining influence. In *maya's* natural state, *sattva* is sometimes in ascendance; at other times *rajas* is in ascendance; or perhaps *tamas* will dominate.

Suppose we had only *rajasic* energy, no *tamasic* or *sattvic* energy. We would be constantly jerking and jumping, moving here and there without control. Say, for illustration's sake, that such *rajasic* people attended a drama held in an auditorium. By the end of the performance the first row of people might have shifted to sit in the last row, and the last row of people might be scattered throughout the auditorium. If there were only rajasic energy would we ever be able to sit still without moving?

Without the principle of *tamas* operating in the phenomenal world, there is no stability-giving energy. Without the energy of *tamas* no one could sit, concentrate on a task or even sleep! But, if there were an over-abundance of *tamas*, we would sit as immobile as a stone. If there were a preponderance of *sattva*, then all 24 hours of the day information would constantly pour in and over-tax our senses. With information constantly cascading into all your senses – the eyes, nose, ears, tongue and skin – you'd be giggling and laughing non-stop. Eventually, this situation would drive you crazy. We require rest from cognitive activity. That rest is given by *maya* operating through the energy of *tamas*.

These three *gunas*, or principles, are *Brahman's* tools used to create, to balance, maintain and dismantle. These tools are also at *our* disposal, for our experiencing and creating. Therefore, let us look upon *maya* or change as a useful instrument.

Seen in another light, *maya* is an "unstable equilibrium" – seemingly a contradiction in terms. Sri Sankaracharya, the 8th-century philosopher who revitalized Hinduism in India, says, "*Maya,* in its creative phase, is a '*vishama avastha*' – an 'unstable equilibrium.'" With *maya* there is always turbulence, dynamic movement, like the acrobat who walks across a tightrope high above the ground carrying an open umbrella. The acrobat constantly wobbles, balancing as he moves along. Similarly, the dynamic of *maya* is an *unstable* equilibrium, ever in motion, ever-changing, ever-balancing.

Sattva is the principle that helps us cognize; *rajas* helps us move, and *tamas* gives us stability. Due to these three principles of *maya* our lives have balance and harmony. However, by disciplining these three energies, we can constantly maintain the ascendancy of *sattva*. We can command the active principle of *rajas* whenever we find it necessary. And we can accept the downward-pulling *tamas* whenever this energy dominates, or we can utilize *tamas* to take a break.

Using Maya *Effectively*

Suppose your child isn't listening to your advice. You ponder the situation, thinking, "I told my son two or three times in a *sattvic* way: 'Please, turn off the television, tomorrow is your exam. If you don't study, you won't pass. And if you don't pass, you won't get into college. Your father and I didn't go to college, so, at least, you must'." Then, what do you do if your child still doesn't respond? You use your *rajas* and become angry. Now you say, firmly, "If you don't turn off the television, you will not have any snacks today." You must express your anger, but as a tool – don't *become* anger. Don't *identify* with the tool. If you *become* anger, then you will overreact and punish your child. Your reaction disturbs the child, and he will start crying. You will start crying, also! Then, after calming down, you will hug your son and say, "Okay, don't study today," whereas the whole purpose of your anger was to persuade him to study! At the end of the argument, your son doesn't end up studying nor are you any more skilled in the art of non-reaction. When you use these tools effectively you bring the entire might of *Brahman* into manifestation in a myriad of ways.

Maya *Expresses That which is Not*

Someone once said that behind the throne of God in heaven, seven angels are dancing on the tip of one needle. Can you imagine it? Impossible! No, nothing is impossible. In fact, I think the number is underestimated; more angels must be dancing on the tip of that needle. When you understand *maya*, you see the infinite, bright possibilities involved! With proper understanding, these three energies in their dynamic equilibrium avail themselves as a tool for your self-expression. *Maya* is ever-changing. *Maya's* three energies (the *gunas*: *sattva*, *rajas* and *tamas*) are dependent upon *Brahman*. From that *maya* all the tools in the world were evolved: the *pancabhutas* (the five subtle elements), their properties, their various combinations – the mind, sense organs, various *lokas*, and various creatures. The entire world of multiplicity is woven out of these three principles.

Let me provide another illustration using the thread garden, to which you were introduced earlier. First, the artist takes a copper wire (that is *tamas*, the stable earth element). Then he winds a thread around the wire (that is *rajas*, activity or movement). Then the thread and wire together are given a certain shape and property (that is *sattva*, form and harmony or balance). Just from these three principles one can create a world of profound experience, but for that you must have both an idea and faith. If you don't have an idea, nothing unfolds. If you have no confidence, what can one accomplish? Faith is expressed as confidence. If you have faith, nothing is impossible.

Maya is a great Creatrix, the manifest *Brahman*. And *She* is ever-changing. She is change itself. You cannot stop the world from changing. Moment to moment, it *moves* – like the Biblical story of creation: "The Spirit of God was *moving* upon the face of the waters" (*Genesis* 1:1). Creation is moving, movement.

Take, for example, a beautiful fabric for which you paid $25.00 a yard. As fabric, it can be used to cover your nakedness. But, once you unravel it, what exactly is that fabric? Fabric is nothing but various strands of colored thread. Thread only presents a possibility. A bundle of thread put lengthwise and crosswise is called fabric. You may call it fabric, but I see it as a bundle of thread. If the thread were unraveled, you would find only fiber. Furthermore, if you unravel the fibers, you would find only fluffy cotton. What do you see in this fluff? Nothing, but from this fluffy cotton someone made fiber, and from that fiber someone made thread. Then someone else kept putting some thread lengthwise and then more thread crosswise, until finally onlookers exclaim, "What a beautiful fabric!" That phenomenon is called *maya*. Actually, if you look at it properly, there is *no* fabric only something we *call* fabric.

Let us retell a well-known folktale, *The Emperor's New Clothes*, with a few modifications for the sake of illustrating the concept of *maya*. According to the story, the Emperor in his royal, resplendent glory was parading down the main street of his capital in the new set of clothes a tailor made for him. When a young boy saw the Emperor parading in his new clothes he exclaimed without hesitation, "The Emperor has no robe! The Emperor is naked!" Meanwhile, everyone else was admiring the "fabrication" and saying, "What a wonderful robe the Emperor is wearing!" It took the unconditioned innocence of a child to penetrate the facade and declare the ultimate truth. Similarly, when we see behind the fabric of *maya*, there is only *Brahman*. You may try to cover yourself with any kind of luxurious fabric, but only an enlightened person with child-like innocence will see: there is only the infinite beauty of *Brahman*.

A Child's Tale of Truth

This story contains a metaphor of enlightenment. Whereas you and I, in our spiritual ignorance, see only our pretenses, the child sees "things as they are." We fail to see through the veil of *maya*; fail to see the fluff behind the woven cloth. That is why we see the Emperor's invisible clothes rather than the Emperor *as he is*! We do not see things as they are, but as composite forms. Fabric is only a myth and metaphor, only a story. If you really analyze, it has no actual existence.

Similarly, take the example of a table. You say, "Oh, here is a beautiful table where I can set my book and cup of tea. What a wonderful design," you exclaim. But if you deeply analyze it, what is the make-up of the table? The table is composed of four legs with a plank on top. The table's composition is only wood. Let us further deconstruct: what is wood? Wood is only tissues. What are tissues? They are only molecules. What are molecules? They are only atoms. What are atoms? They are protons, electrons and neutrons. What are protons, electrons and neutrons? Finally you resist probing further: "Swami, do we need to go to that extent?" You suggest instead, "Let's have a cup of tea," favoring indulgence over the discovery of Truth behind the veil of *maya*.

An Etymological Definition of Maya

Such illustrations help us to understand why another definition of *maya* is "*ya ma sa maya*." "*Ma*" means "not." "*Maya* is that which is *not*." From a physicist's standpoint, an object, such as a table, is only a dancing set of atoms. As such, there is *no* table. These are the great teachings of the *Upanishadic rishis* as well as the Buddha. And still, you can utilize the principle of *maya* on the relative level of consciousness. But if you go deeper and deeper, your perception of the world totally changes.

This *Law of Maya* is explained as "*ya ma sa maya*" – the etymological meaning of *maya* – "that which does not exist." Both the form and the function are *maya*. Why is the function *maya*? For someone the table may be useful as a place to set a book. Someone else may use the table as a place to sit. Of what use is the table for the person who has neither a book nor a need to sit? He will see the wood from the table as wonderful firewood and dream of using it that way, too!

That is why we call the material world *maya*. The particular function of a table, or any object of perception is relative to the person who perceives it. We bring our own perceptions to objects and situations. One person will see the utility of a particular object. Other people will bring other meanings and perceptions, different utilities to various objects and situations.

For example, if I were to give a *Bhagavad Gita* to several different people, free, some people would read it everyday, religiously. Others would cover it with a beautiful leather case, stamp their personal seal on every page, write their name in big letters on the inside page, and then place the book very prominently inside the living room bookcase so that anybody walking by cannot escape seeing it. A third person might puzzle, "What will I do with this?" – and decide to market it. In his mind, he even generates a promotional sales talk: "The *Bhagavad Gita* is the most wonderful thing. You know, Warren Hastings once remarked, 'The Empire upon which the sun never sets may disappear, but this *Bhagavad Gita* will never disappear'," and he imagines selling thousands. His actual client agrees, "Okay, I'll buy it," and then wonders to himself, "If it's such a wonderful book, why isn't he keeping it?" A fourth person sees the *Bhagavad Gita*, and, using it as a pillow, gets good sleep!

These four types of people bring very different perceptions, values, emotions and responses to the same phenomena. Different structures rise to the surface of their perception. For those who want to sleep, *Bhagavad Gita* makes a wonderful pillow. That individual doesn't see a glorious scripture there, just an ordinary pillow. Another person sees money in the bank:

"What possibilities! So much money can come my way! I'll not just sell one *Gita*, but millions all over the world!" A third person sees personal glory – "I possess this famous and glorious *Gita*. When everyone sees that I own it and how well I have kept it, the *Gita's* glory will be transferred onto me. They will recognize me as a great philosopher. Let me keep this *Gita* where everyone will notice." This individual sees a claim to glory, name and fame in the *Gita*. It is only a very small percentage of humanity who sees the opportunity to gain wisdom by studying the *Gita*.

This is why I say that material and psychological structures, objects and situations, are a myth. Different people harvest different sensations and experiences from what exists. Hence, "*ya ma sa maya*" – "*maya* is that which is not there." Different individuals perceive the same object or situation (structure) differently. Ten people harvest ten different experiences from an object or a situation. None will experience it in exactly the same way.

Maya's *Magical Projecting Power*

Therefore, we may say that *maya* creates. She is a Creatrix. "*Aghadita ghadana padiyasi maya*," (Sankaracharya's *Mayapanchakam*): "*Maya* is capable of creating impossible things." It brings joy – if one is aware of *maya's* power. If you are *un*aware, *maya* is a source of suffering. Because of its ever-changing nature and ability to combine itself in a million ways, *maya* has infinite creative power. She is a magician.

Have you seen how a magician works? He brings a hollow cylinder, covers himself completely in a black flowing gown, and holds a "magic" wand in his hand. As he jumps up on the stage, he waves the wand, and your eyes follow wherever his wand sways to and fro. The waving of the wand both attracts and disturbs your vision. Your mind is no longer fixed but has become distracted. Then the magician flutters a black veil, and you see everything black and blurry. From under the veil, the magician draws out the cylinder and demonstrates that it is hollow at both ends. To prove that it is empty, he asks someone to put their hand through the cylinder. After the subject finds nothing inside, the magician puts the cylinder on the table, waves his wand again and a plethora of scarves, white rabbits, clothes, vessels, toys, chocolates, and even an ice cream cone appear. You wonder, "Where did he get all this?" By creating confusion in your mind, the *mayavi* – the magician – has covertly transferred something into the cylinder without your noticing and now he pulls it out.

Such is *maya's* great power of projection. If we understand that power of projection, a power which we all possess, the world is a very interesting experience. If we don't understand the power of *maya*, then the world is very confusing and puzzling.

Maya *as Measure*

"*Ya ma sa maya*" has another meaning. *Ma* can also mean "measure," like a gallon or a bushel. A bushel provides the farmer a kind of measure. Suppose a farmer has a heap of paddy (rice with its husk). This heap of paddy is a non-quantified mass of grain. The farmer has no idea how much paddy he has. Then he brings a bushel basket and scoops the paddy into it until it is full, and then tilts the bushel basket, pouring out the paddy, and finally measures how many bushels of paddy he has – one bushel, then a second, third and fourth. Within half an hour he discovers how much paddy he has, how much it will bring him, and how far his agricultural efforts have been successful.

However, this *Field of Infinite Potentialities* differs from paddy. This *Field* is homogeneous, immeasurable, non-quantifiable and invisible Pure Consciousness. Using *maya* as a measure, you size up your infinitude in the form of myriad structures, combinations and functions. *Maya* is a structuring process. *Maya* provides us with a measuring mechanism. As an instrument of measure, *maya* reveals the potentiality latent in *Brahman*. *Maya* is a measure of the Immeasurable. By itself, the Immeasurable cannot be completely measured, but *maya*, being the ever-changing modification of the three *gunas*, can generate manifold structures from itself for unfolding our spiritual potential. When our thoughts formulate, they take myriad forms. Our consciousness flows into ideas, into functions and into created things. *Maya* acts as a "measure" or channel of the Immeasurable, measuring out or channeling *Brahman* into the material world, making stellar constellations, the rain forest and the brain of a newborn.

Is and Is Not

Another of Sankara's definitions of *maya* is "*sat asat bhyam anirvachaniya maya.*" What does "*sat asat bhyam avirvachaniya maya*" mean? *Sat* means "existence, an existing object; something that is." *Asat* means "non-existent; something which is not." Sankara says that you cannot put *maya* in either of these categories. You cannot say whether *maya* exists, nor can you say that *maya* does not exist.

Certain things you can definitely say do not exist. What are those? "Please draw a square circle. If you can't draw one, please try, at least, to conceive of a square circle in your mind – a kind of Zen Buddhist *koan.*" This exercise will tease your brain quite a lot and, ultimately, you may fall asleep! You simply cannot conceive of a square circle. There are word combinations, such as "square circle," but they don't refer to anything. Words which do not refer to anything are empty. Such objects don't exist, and we call that category *asat* – non-existent.

For example, see the table standing before you. Does the table exist? Now, with a little more knowledge of *maya*, you have probably become cautious about answering. You cannot be sure. In order to respond, you now understand the need to know the precise definition of existence. Existence is "that which *always* is and does not change during all the three periods of time (past, present, future)." Existence is infinite and, therefore, must be there all the time. If we take that definition – "existence is that which exists in all the three periods of time" – then can you say the table, standing before you, exists? You cannot say that it exists because the table changes. Then can you say the table standing in front of you is non-existent? No, you cannot, because you see the table, use it and touch it. Then what is the table? *Maya*. It neither exists nor non-exists – "*sat asat bhyam avirvachaniya maya*." Such instances, which cannot be put in absolute black-and-white terms, constitute the analytical method we use to understand *maya*.

Existence and non-existence flow into each other creating a third category we call *maya* or *mithya*. We cannot categorize objects as either existing or non-existing. Objects, like a "square circle," that we have neither seen nor can we imagine, even in our dreams, are "absolutely non-existent" (*atyanta abhava*). Other objects we can see and touch, and, therefore, we cannot dismiss them as non-existent. But, at some earlier time these objects did not exist. And we can also completely dismantle or destroy them – e.g. use the table as firewood and it disappears as a table. Or, in time, an object decays and disintegrates on its own. How do we classify such objects of experience? We say, "It is *maya*" – both existing and non-existing. *Maya* is that power which cannot be determined either as "is or is not."

A Dream Existence

So, "*svakale satyavad bhadi prabhode sadi asat bhavet,*" – "When I experience it, it is there, when I don't experience it, it is not there" (*Atmabodh.* 6). Sometimes you experience an object, but upon further investigation, it is not there – for example, your dreams. In dreams all of us may become Amitabh Bacchans or Tom Hanks, Vajpaiyees, or Bushes, or Tatas or Rockefellers. We become them, because we admire such people! The more we admire someone or something, the more we become that. In dream we create our own private worlds. We become whatever we want. But when we wake up from that dream, we are not that. Doesn't it happen like that? Since the dream is not there when you awaken, can you give it any reality? Still, while you were dreaming, the experience was very real – the way you were addressing the Congress or Parliament! When? In your dream: the way you were preparing lectures and ideas to address the onslaught of your opposition! Then you heard the sound of a shot and thought, "Terrorists have attacked!" Then, suddenly, you wake up and the dream world dissolves. Just as a dream, the table standing in front of you, or the fabric you wear can neither be true or untrue. This phenomenon is an "in-between" category, an indescribable puzzle. One who thinks deeply is unable to categorically say that an object or experience is either existing or non-existing. That is why Sankara says, "*visvam tyaktva svapnavicharam*," "Detach from this dream world" (*Bhajagovindam*. 23).

Once, you were in college and everyone danced around you admiringly whispering, "She's bound to become a cinema star." Now, you are 90 years old, all shriveled-up and your teeth are missing. Baldness is slowly creeping-up. You are deaf and bent over with osteoporosis. When some old friend reminds you of your college days, how will you react? "Don't embarrass me by saying all those things. I, too, once believed that was true. Now I understand that it was only a myth, a momentary dream without a foundation. I had built a castle in the sand." When you were young, if somebody had told you that existence is all *maya*, you would have exclaimed, "She's just jealous of me," or, "He just pretends not to appreciate my good looks." Previously, you never understood the meaning of *maya*, that those dreams and experiences were only a thought. Now, with your understanding you can see your youth *and* old age, the beginning and the end in one singular vision – you realize both are *mithya, maya*. You can freely admit, "Once I was a young and beautiful girl, and now I am an old and shriveled-up woman." All these stages and events are *mithya*, unreal, illusory, *maya*. What is true is beyond all this. Once you make this realization, you can enjoy both and be playful.

When you are a young beautiful woman, you spread beauty

and fragrance all around and when you are an old woman, you spread the beauty of your experience, your wisdom, your love. Both are enjoyable experiences. That attitude helps us to move with the rhythm of *maya*. "Roll with every punch." Haven't you heard that saying? When you are in a gymnasium fighting, and your opponent gives you a punch, you had better dodge and roll with the punch – particularly in Kerala's martial arts! Don't resist. If you resist, you will be pulverized. Dance and roll and dodge. This is how you move with the flow of *maya*. *Maya* is a powerful flow. Life is only a dream; experience is perceptual and cannot be categorized as either Real or unreal: "*Ma kuru dhana jana yavana garvam haradi nimeshad kalasarvam / maya mayamidam akhilam buddhva brahmapadam tvam pravisha vididtva*" (*Bhajagovindam*. 11). "Don't identify with wealth, relatives, your youth or your physical beauty – all those can be lost in a second. Knowing that all those are *maya*, may you realize *Brahman*." Life is a flow; your body is a flow. We are a constant flow.

The Flow of Existence

Modern scientists say that your body is made up of many trillion cells. You can add a couple of hundreds one way or another. No matter. These trillions of cells that constitute your body are further made up of an unimaginable number of dancing atoms. Every six hours, one-fourth of those atoms migrate from you to other objects. That is why we have the *sandhya vandana* – that is, *pranayama* and the chanting of the *Gayatri mantra* every six hours. The atoms move from where they were and go elsewhere. Meanwhile, another set of atoms come to abide in you. Then, after six hours, another set departs, etc. Every 24 hours you are a completely different bag of atoms, a changed person. That is why Buddha said, "The body is like a river. You cannot step into the same river twice. The river, into which you stepped yesterday or even a moment ago, is not the river that you step in today."

Likewise, the same person cannot be seen twice. When I first met you at the beginning of the lecture and the one whom I see at the end of the lecture is entirely different, from the atomic standpoint. You have become a totally different set of atoms! You came in alive and bubbling, but, by the end of the lecture, everyone is sleepy. *Tamas* overtook you. It is a change, and *it is welcome*. Every change is welcome. If you didn't change, that would be most problematic. Every six hours the atoms in the body change. Life is a flow, like a flame on the tip of the lamp, constantly metamorphosing. The body is changing. The world outside is constantly changing. Is there anything that is unchanging? People change, objects change, even stars change. After 5 billion years the sun will burn up, exhausting all its energy and finally collapse into an insignificant black hole. That is the sun's fate – to become a piece of charcoal. Then something else happens as a result of that change.

We constantly change. Things outside us change. On the physiological level things are changing. Once upon a time you were very healthy. Now your kidneys don't function, your heart valves are corroded, and your liver is fatty and inefficient. Nothing functions. A stage comes when you decide to quit. Are your thoughts the same as they were when you were young, or even the same as last week? They keep on changing.

Maya, *the Inexplicable*

Once there were two lunatics in an asylum, and a stranger came to see them. The stranger asked one man, "How did you get here?" He answered, "It is a sad tale. I could not marry the woman I loved." The stranger sympathized with him and then turned to the other man and asked, "How did you happen to end up here?" The other man responded, "I married that woman." How is it possible that one man did *not* marry a particular woman and go crazy and another man married her and went crazy? Without the woman he loved, one man went mad, and, another man, having married that same woman became a lunatic! *Maya* is inexplicable.

Sankara says, "*Anirvachaniya maya,*" – "you just cannot explain it," either man's position. Both are mad but the causes are different. They bring different perspectives, different experiences, and they harvest different pleasures or results. Both loved the same woman; one went crazy because he didn't marry her and the other because he did marry her. What else can you say? It goes beyond our reasoning. We just don't understand. That is the puzzle of life. When you look at it from the various angles, experience is a jigsaw puzzle that can never be solved – *unless* you bring these laws into play.

Once, there was a very powerful king who ruled a large kingdom and lived in a great palace, amidst its very wealthy capital, along with a big army, institutions, and court full of ministers and advisors. One day, after his lunch, he went to his master bedroom for a post-lunch siesta. While sleeping that afternoon the king had a dream that he had become a butterfly. A dream has its own reality and the king felt that he really was a butterfly. Even if someone in the dream had told him, "You are not a butterfly, but a king," he wouldn't have believed it. In the dream, the butterfly was sitting beside a pond. Suddenly a frog whipped his tongue out and tried to snatch the butterfly. The butterfly struggled to get free and, in the process, lost both of its wings. But somehow it escaped a worse fate – being lapped up in the frog's mouth. The wingless butterfly fell down, and, as it dropped, the king suddenly woke up.

When the king opened his eyes, he found himself lying down in his master bedroom. He checked his hands, his robes, and his crown. No problem; they were all in place. Then a thought crept into his mind, "Just a while ago I was a butterfly, but now I am the king lying down in the king's master bedroom of the palace. Which of these two am I, actually? Am I a butterfly, or am I a king? Then he called his minister and asked, "Tell me, am I a butterfly or a king?" The Minister sobbed, "Sir, what has happened to you? Before you went to sleep you were a normal person." The king continued, "Just a while ago I was a butterfly, but now I am the king." The minister pleaded, "Sir, how can you say that you are a butterfly? Can't you see you are a king?" The king retorted, "But what about that butterfly?" His minister sighed, "That was only your dream!" The king said, "How so? Perhaps the notion that I am a king is a dream of the butterfly." Now, the minister shook his head in utter despair.

What the truth is, I don't know. Maybe the post-butterfly phase king is the dream of that butterfly. I'm not sure. Nor can anyone be sure about whether that butterfly was the dream of the king or the king was the dream of the butterfly. No one can say with certainty – "*Sat asat bhyam anirvachaniya maya*" – "it neither exists nor non-exists." One can only marvel at the way the *maya* flows and brings out incredible varieties of existence. That is all we can say. Before you realize it, things have changed.

Change – an Opportunity to Express your Potential

Within seconds things can change. You should be prepared for change. That is the idea. The *Bhagavad Gita*, says, "*Janma–mrtyu-jara-vyadhi-duhkha-dos'anudarsanam.*" You must be ready for continuous change – "birth, growth, old age, disease, suffering and finally death" (13:8). When someone dies, why do you say that you are "shocked"? Why are you shocked? Was there a loose electric wire? It is a *Law of Nature* that the born must die. One should be ready for constant change. Be prepared. When you have that attitude, you can manifest your full potential in any situation.

When Bhishma lay upon his deathbed made of arrows, Dharmaputra, the eldest Pandava beseeched him, "Give us a lecture on *dharma*." Was that the time to ask the dying patriarch this question? Bhishma did not burst out, saying, "You ungrateful wretch, coming at this time to bother me, not even offering me a glass of water and then asking me these kinds of questions!" He did not argue or fuss, because he applied this *Law of Change*: "Once upon a time I was seated on the throne surrounded by servants, but today I am lying on a bed of arrows. This is the march of *Maya*. Let me submit to it." When you submit to the *Law of Maya* you will also be able to invoke your potential. Bhishma made his best presentation and expression of himself. Nothing could stop him. In fact, that condition was required for expressing his potential!

De-conditioning – a Tool of Maya

Does it surprise you that in such a condition we can unfold our potential? That is the meaning of accepting *maya*, the meaning of flowing with constant change. The *Law of Maya* suggests that we keep moving, innovate, be new, renew – continuously. Don't bring the old memories to understand the present situation. The situation has already changed. Most often we bring our old experiences and our prior conditionings along. When we meet a person, we immediately judge him – "I think he is a rascal!" How do you know? "I just think so." You bring an old attitude along. Perhaps he looks like your uncle with the big mustache who pinched your cheeks hard when you were a baby, and you subtly remember that aggression. In your mind, this uncle's mustache is connected with displeasure, so whenever you see a man with a mustache, your blood pressure goes up and you think of that person as your adversary.

The more you bring the past into understanding the present, the more you miss immediate contact and fail to live in touch with the present. That is the meaning of old age and death – you are no longer able to understand the present. With a mind full of cobwebs, you are unable to *un*learn, or to *dis*-identify with the past. To that extent you remain steeped and battered and conditioned by memories. You miss the glory, the beauty, the dynamism and the vitality of the present. Therefore, keep moving; don't bring the same old attitude to the new people and situations that you meet. Understand everyone as having infinite potential. Without condemnation, see everyone as *Shiva*, as the Lord, and give them another opportunity to present themselves, to correct themselves.

The dynamic of bringing the old worn-out past to fresh

circumstances becomes what they call self-fulfilling prophecy: "Didn't I tell you that you would fail your examination?" Sometimes children are afraid and say, "Mom, I am going to fail." Or you tell them, and when it becomes true you are quick to state your claim to fame, "Didn't I tell you!" This attitude becomes a self-fulfilling prophecy. Don't engage in that behavior or condition the present using attitudes from the past. Be free, move along with change. To the extent that we are capable of going with the flow and running with *maya*, we can use Her as an instrument, as a structure and as a tool for exploring and expressing our individual potential.

Brahman – *Ever-New, Ever-Renewing Source of All*

Brahman is described as "*navam*" – always new. Things are always new; it is only our ideas, thoughts and perceptions that don't change with change. Everything else, around us and within us, changes. If we understand this law and apply it in our lives we become flexible, fluid, unresisting in our constant willingness to accept change. When we are able to flow with *maya*, flow with the various structures that *She* creates, then these ever-dynamic and complex structures become the tools for you to explore and express your potential.

The *Vedantin* is always ready to change. He will even change his opinion about himself! One ought to develop a willingness to change. Innovate, look at things freshly and bring new ideas into understanding and coping with the present. Just for the joy of it we ought to change. One should make this ideal a religion. Adopt the attitude, "I will change *just* for the sake of changing" – not that every person is asking you to change.

Most of the time people are happy simply the way they are. Even you appreciate the *status quo* – "Everyone is enjoying me the way I am, so why should I change?" We don't want to lose a winning game, change our pattern of playing in this world. When change is suggested, you argue, "I am feeling comfortable with myself!" That is the problem. We want everyone else to change, but are we ready to change ourselves? "Why should I?" you retort. "Let everybody else adjust." Unless *you* are willing to change, you will never be able to motivate others to change themselves. That willingness becomes very important.

Like Bhishma, we ought to be prepared to apply that law moment to moment. That willingness to experiment, not just stay put in the routine, is characteristic of the person who understands *maya*, who understands that everything is constantly changing. Life offers a new design everyday – a situation which is very difficult for most of us to accept. It means that we have to be very alert all the time. Most often we are very happy to walk the trodden path. But the truth is that when we walk the trodden path, we manage to get around easily – but we slowly become somnambulists, robots! Everything is done "in your sleep"! You cease to enjoy what you are doing because you are doing everything mechanically. How will you introduce any newness in this kind of life?

Renounce and Announce

Make change a religion. Want change. Continue to change and grow. That is the way to discover one's self. A commitment to change ought to become a veritable religion for you. As an example, at the end of the *Mahabharata*, Arjuna wanted Krishna to explain the *Bhagavad Gita* once again. Arjuna begged, "Please repeat whatever you told me in the battlefield." Krishna responded, "I never repeat; I keep on changing. At that time I told you to fight. Now, if you ask me I may tell you not to fight but to meditate instead. Depending upon the situation, I may change. My opinions, responses and teachings are unpredictable." Krishna – or any realized person who is in touch with *Brahman* – is unpredictable. Such a person is ever-changing, ever-renewed, ever-responsive and spontaneous.

Three

The Spiritual Law of Dharma

Experiencing our Uniqueness

The third law is the *Law of Dharma*. What is the meaning of *dharma*? *"Dharanat dharmamityahu,"* meaning "*dharma* is that which sustains life." The *Law of Dharma* states that every individual is unique and has a unique personality, mission and destiny. We all are unique beings. When you reflect upon life, you recognize that you have experienced this uniqueness. All of us have self-experience, the quality of just being my-"self," yourself, himself or herself. Being here and now in this situation, as an individual entity, as the one who responds to and engages in experience, who works, thinks, doubts, listens to music or reads a book, is our present experience. That experience distinguishes us from each other and makes us unique. Uniqueness is what defines experience.

There are billions of people in this world. You may be lost in a crowd, or everyone may forget you, but can you ever lose yourself? In the airport terminal, someone holds up a placard with your name written on it to identify you, because otherwise no one recognizes you. But after you exit the airport, do you need an ID card for your self-identification in these unfamiliar surroundings?

We each have a sense of our "selves" that we never lose. We know that we are unique persons. We may compare ourselves with another person, "I am stupid, and she is intelligent," distinguish ourselves from others, exchange our experiences – demonstrating that the experience of ourselves is unique, something that the individual alone knows. An individual means a phenomenon that cannot be replicated. Self-experience is both private and unique. No one can know you beyond a limit. Even husband and wife, after forty years of marriage, sit down together and mutually admit, "I have yet to really understand you." Understanding one another is an endless pursuit. More often that not, we fail to convey our uniqueness to others. The problem is that sometimes we don't even understand ourselves! No one can devise a standard for our private experiences. Rather, each of us is a standard unto ourselves.

An individual means one who is indivisible. We may compare notes, but we cannot deconstruct self-experience. There is a certain non-negotiable, indivisible, indissoluble individuality about us. That is what makes us persons. Otherwise, we would have been puppets or robots. We are neither. But as persons, we must know *who* we are – a challenge which is different from either being objects or animals.

When you explore the *Upanishadic* literature, you discover

that you are *Sat-chit-ananda*, you are that Spirit, that *Field of Infinite Potentialities.* We may understand the *Upanishadic* statement intellectually, but such knowledge does not give us a sense of our full selfhood. There may be a grand ground from whence we all spring, but we also have to deal with our unique individuality.

Thus, it becomes important to understand our uniqueness, learn to cultivate it and explore the world through self-expression. Most of us go through situations where we try to cut corners, fashion ourselves, like a carpenter making a cabinet. First the carpenter gathers his tools and materials, cuts the wood into appropriate sizes and shapes, and then pieces them together building a cabinet. A cabinet is an artificial object and can be dismantled at anytime.

What the carpenter does with wood, we do to ourselves: cut down, shape and condition, fit and fix. The more we try to do that, the more neurotic we become. The more we try to conform to situations, the more complexes we develop. As a result, we have become hypocrites. This kind of attempt is the primary reason for human madness. When you understand your uniqueness, then you know what you should do in any circumstance – what your mission in life is and what is expected of you.

First of all, let us accept this law that declares that each individual is unique. Knowing what makes you unique will help you in understanding and in developing your self-expression; whereas the lack of self-knowledge will limit your unique self-expression and contribution to the world.

"My" Dharma

We begin our inquiry into the nature and the *Law of Dharma* by asking this question: "What is my *dharma* – my uniqueness?" The *Bhagavad Gita* begins with the word *dharma* and ends with the word "*mama*." If we put together the first and the last words of *Bhagavad Gita*, they formulate this question, "What is my *dharma*?" Your *dharma* is not my *dharma*, because we are unique individuals. Each of us has to resolve this question within ourselves and decide. Others may try to tell you, "This is your *dharma*, what you are expected to do," but ultimately it is your responsibility to decide what your *dharma* is, who you are and what to do with your life.

Particularly in crisis situations, we ask, "What is my *dharma*? How do I define myself and the standard by which I determine my responses?" For example, when terrorists destroyed the World Trade Center and crashed into the Pentagon, the President and the people of America agonized over this question of *dharma* – how to respond to this terrible crisis. They questioned deeply: "Who are we, and what should we do? What is our *dharma* – as a nation; as individuals; as a father or mother; as a firefighter or emergency worker; or as the President of the

United States; or even as a member of a diverse, global community?

Although you are an individual, you are also a parent, or may be the President of the United States! You are required to deal with conflicting values and considerations. Taking into account all the dynamics of a situation, you determine an appropriate response. It's impossible to simply read the "bluebook" and come up with a ready-made response. One has to bring all the impinging factors into consideration. Moment to moment the question arises – "What exactly is my *dharma*?" With numerous and even conflicting concerns in mind, you arrive at a decision, and that decision is an expression of your uniqueness.

Though I may be someone's son or daughter, the *Law of Dharma* declares, "I am unique. I am distinct from my parents and have my own individuality." Just as parents have their own individuality, children also have their own uniqueness. Every child coming into this world has a mouth for eating, a mind for thinking, and a pair of hands to work. When you reflect upon your individuality, your own uniqueness, you feel like a flower in a garden. In a garden you find different flowers. No flower is exactly the same as any other flower. There is always some difference in pattern and color, in their variety of size and fragrance, in the contrast they bring to a garden.

Flowers are not like manufactured matchboxes. Every matchbox that rolls out of a match factory is identical. You can pick up any matchbox and see that they are all the same size and shape, and the same color, and each box has the same number of matchsticks. There is no difference at all. But compare two individuals' thumb impressions; even if they are twins there will be a difference! God's creation is forever unique. That being the case – that we *all* are unique individuals – then we have to define the meaning and nuances of *dharma* around this key concept.

Needs and Talents

As unique individuals, we bring unique talents, *sahaja prakriti*, one's inborn nature, into this world. Along with these talents we also bring a set of needs, though we may pretend not to have such needs! We often state our needs obliquely or in veiled language. But, when we are pushed to the wall, we express them forcefully as our own non-negotiable needs. What is important is matching our needs with our talents while interacting in a given situation.

You are not the only unique individual! You find yourself surrounded by many such unique individuals, who have their own needs and talents, are trying to find their niche! We are trying to interact and explore the possibility of jointly growing and unfolding our potential. It is not that you alone exist and the world is at your service. Every individual is trying to find a niche for himself in this dialogical world, full of others who are likewise exploring their niche. Consequently, our lives become very interdependent and complex. The more I accommodate your needs and talents in my pursuit, the more I become clear about and discover my *dharma* and my destiny.

None of us will compromise beyond a point. Even in your interaction with your spouse or children, with your parents, or co-workers and friends, your compromising has a limit. If your own son hurts your personal interests, or your parental or individual feelings, you are apt to suggest, "Son, Why do you continue to hang around me? Why don't you go to Mumbai, settle there and make a life for yourself?" Ironically, this is the same father whom you will also hear say, "I am old, son; please come and stay with me. Don't you know it's your duty to serve me in my old age?" Even a mother, who is the symbol of total sacrifice and unconditional love, will not tolerate you beyond a limit. When you touch her dignity and respect, her core individuality, she will shout, "Get out of my house," because there is a limit beyond which she cannot compromise her needs. In each one of us, that core set of needs has to be recognized. And if you recognize it, that is better for you.

You may dialogue with your marriage partner or with your children, or friends and colleagues, but most of the time you either don't recognize or fail to admit your own core needs. We feel a little shy about expressing our non-negotiable needs: "How can I say what my needs are?" Since every *guru* extols the renunciation of all your desires, reducing your needs, and advises continuously sacrificing yourself for the other, you legitimately question, "Then, how do I deal with self-expression? How can I say that these are my needs?" Even as a guest in a home, we generally are reserved about stating our needs. You know that you prefer a cup of tea without sugar, but you will not say that. When your hostess brings a cup of tea brimming with sugar, you feel obligated and accept it with a reluctant smile.

It is better that you state your needs. Otherwise, inwardly you are unhappy while outwardly you only pretend to be happy. As a result you develop inner conflicts and become schizophrenic. When there is no inner smile, even though you try smiling, it is a very laborious exercise. You don't feel like smiling, but you oblige. Rarely do we have the honesty to admit our innermost needs.

Once you express your needs, you must become responsible for them, *and* you must also be honest about your talents. Suppose a *swami* brags, "I can recite the whole *Gita*." Then his devotee speaks up, "Okay, let's chant the *Gita* together." After all, a *swami* is supposed to know how to chant the entire *Gita*, but this particular *swami* actually only knew the 12th and 15th chapters! He never expected that someone would request him to chant the whole of it! Generally, when we brag, no one asks us to carry it out.

Such claims become a big responsibility. First of all, you are dishonest about your talent, and you hide that fact. Or you don't want to admit your lack of knowledge. Or perhaps you just don't want to disclose what your real talents are. As a consequence of your failure to be responsible about stating your needs and lack of honesty in presenting your talents, your relationships suffer. If you don't place your needs and talents on the table, you're forced to become manipulative or dishonest.

Generally, most of the words we use to communicate are used to hide our genuine needs. Since we rarely communicate our list of non-negotiable needs, we end up trying to manipulate others. For example, you want to go to a particular movie, but you don't want to admit it. Instead, you cleverly ask your friend or spouse, "What are you doing this evening?" He or she replies, "I don't have any plans." Then you think that this is your chance and say: "There is a good movie showing that you would enjoy." But who is it that really wants to see the film? You do! But, for you own reasons, you avoid being forthright. Slowly you manipulate your friend or spouse into a decision to see the film with you, and then you say you are being diplomatic! That's a novel definition of diplomacy. Furthermore, in the long run, that sort of diplomacy will not sustain! We need to understand one another. Diplomacy means using direct communication and incorporating your counterpart's needs together with your needs, rather than using manipulative techniques to *trick* others into meeting your needs! When you communicate your needs properly, listen to the other person's needs and then decide matters, you become a true diplomat – one who is sensitive to another person's needs.

To accept that we are unique persons and that we all have our own needs is important to our human dignity. That unique need is to be expressed. "This is *my* need; beyond that limit I cannot go." That is the *meaning of honesty*! If your needs are not fulfilled, you may rationalize waiting for sometime. But, beyond a point, if they are not fulfilled, you explode! When you explode you become violent or even homicidal. Otherwise you implode. When you implode you become an introvert, a suicide, or a mental wreck, and you operate on a joyless, low level of efficiency. You manage day-to-day life, but there is no sense of fulfillment.

When the dynamic of expressing your needs and incorporating the other's interests in your projects is understood, you also understand the need to develop these two skills – sensitivity towards the other and communication – and that is what is called *dharma*. I have to put my needs on the table, you also put yours, and that way we can negotiate. When we put our needs on the table and negotiate, we become non-violent individuals. Recognizing another's needs while communicating our needs is the meaning of non-violence, *ahimsa*. Manipulation of the other is *himsa*, violence.

Growing in Association

Most of us find that there is no fulfillment either in our home or work life. Our occupational and our marriage relationships often give an appearance of satisfaction and harmony, but are you enjoying and growing as a person? Do you feel that you are unfolding your powers? No. You feel locked up, boxed into a situation, and don't know what to do. When your *guru* asks, "How's everything?" you answer lifelessly, "Swamiji, I'm carrying on. Nothing very important or exciting." You lack energy to do anything, and the reason is because, from the very beginning, you did not say exactly what you wanted from the relationship or contract with another. Without acknowledging what your needs and the other person's needs are, how can a common understanding develop? How can you discover a common ground so that, jointly, both of you can grow? "*Saha dharmam caratha*" – "Let us walk together on the path of righteousness." This line is recited in Hindu marriage ceremonies That is the basis and meaning of marriage: we are trying to mutually grow in our association with one another. As we mutually grow in relationship, the unique needs and talents of each person are expressed and fulfilled.

Let me tell a story: Thinking his son was useless, Hastamalaka's father declared, "I renounce you," and Hastamalaka was gifted to Sankaracharya. But, unlike the boy's father, Sankaracharya saw an extraordinary individual. He had the ability to recognize the intelligence and unlock the uniqueness of this child. Sankaracharya asked Hastamalaka only one relevant, philosophical question, "Child, who are you?" The question stirred Hastamalaka, whose name means, "For whom Truth is like a berry in the hollow of his hand," and the child responded by writing a wonderful composition, "*Hastamalakiyam*" meaning, "Song of the Self." Sankara, himself, was impressed by the profundity of the boy, and wrote a commentary on Hastamalaka's song. And Hastamalaka became one of the greatest disciples of Sankara and a spiritual master.

Today, we have devised standardized intelligent tests, but those are an inadequate means by which to measure someone's *real* intelligence. The "idiot-boy" was talented, but others saw him through the same old standard lens that they used for everyone. They possessed no standard by which to discover another's uniqueness, excellence and genius. Whereas, Hastamalaka's genius went unrecognized in one environment and situation, new associations allowed him to flourish, and his genius finally became recognized.

Similarly, there are people lying idly, gazing at butterflies and the sunset or the moonrise, whom we think are useless, until one day they come out with something wonderful – like the author of the book, *God of Small Things*, or *The Wasteland*, which inspired and challenged the world. Overnight the author becomes a celebrity. When Milton was writing *Paradise Lost*, nobody recognized his existence, said nothing of his talent.

But when he became famous, several claims get made: "He was born here, in my city!" "He lived in this very house that I now own!"

With all this variety in the world, we require and have our own unique place or role. Consequently, we ask, "What is my *dharma*, my duty in this world? What is my mission, and what is my place? Why am I here?" These questions constantly nag us, and yet very few people discover an answer to these questions. Most of us are blind to our mission, or like headless chickens we go about running here and there aimlessly. By the time we discover our mission we are so old that we conclude, "Swamiji, I need one more life to apply all this information and wisdom that I have gained."

Contextual Dharma

Sankaracharya in his commentary to the Introduction of the *Bhagavad Gita*, defines *dharma* as "*Jagatah sthiti karanam praninam abhyudaya nishreyasa hetuh varnibhih ashramabhih shreyo'arthibhih anushtiyamanah dharma.*" "*Dharma* is a system of discipline meant to maintain order in the world (*jagatah sthiti karanam*) and to promote spiritual and material well-being of all creatures (*praninam abhyudaya nishreyasa hetuh*), and to be practiced by people according to their psychological disposition and station in society (*varna*) and their stage in life (*ashrama*)."

As we jointly work and explore, what is required to be developed is an understanding of *dharma*. At this level of discovery and application, *dharma* means moral and ethical disciplines, certain virtues. As a result of practicing these disciplines you will be able to integrate everyone's interests and then mutually grow. "*Sangacadhvam samvadadhvam samvomanamsi janatham.*" "United we walk, united we speak and united we feel and think" (*Rig Veda* 10:191-2). Progress in isolation will be very anemic and unhealthy. What you require is progress in the context of everyone's progress.

The existence and needs of the other define your context. This context requires the matching of two demands – your talents and needs. That adds to the complexity of the situation which is rarely under your control. Therefore, *dharma* requires that we "promote the common good" – *jagadah sthiti karanam* – and the "well-being of all creatures" – *praninam abhyudaya nishreyas hetu*. First of all, your actions must contribute to and maintain your environment. In the civil society, certain civic amenities are required – adequate roads, a good educational system, hospitals, a constitutional framework for government and a society ruled by law. These are the general environmental conditions we want to preserve. Then only can we explore our potential – individually and collectively. If those conditions are not fulfilled, we cannot live as a *dharma purusha* – a *dharmic* being. When the system is defective, everyone becomes corrupt; even good people will be *adharmic* – unrighteous, avoiding paying their taxes, skirting the law of the land, etc. We should see that our acts contribute to the maintenance of the civil society governed by law and order.

The performance of your duties, your life and life's work, should contribute to the spiritual and material affluence of the society. This applies not only to you, but also to people as a whole, and not merely to our *material* well-being, but also to our *spiritual* well-being – meaning the opportunity to grow and unfold without hindrance, along with a deep sense of satisfaction.

Rights and Wrongs

If your activities do not contribute to the general well-being of the world, something is wrong in what you do. You must pause, think, pray and fast. Your deep contemplation might go something like this: "What I am doing hurt many people. I will not be able to follow my destiny in such a hostile environment that develops on account of my actions. I have to adjust so that all of us can pursue our bliss in our own unique ways." As an old aphorism says, "You have the right to swing your walking stick, but your rights end where the other man's nose begins!" You can swing freely up to the point of hurting another. Beyond that your freedom impinges upon others' freedom. Sensitivity to the other person's existence is a necessary virtue. Otherwise, if you hit him, he will snatch your stick and exercise his equal right to swing back!

If I pluck out one of your eyes, you will pluck out both my eyes. I knock out one of your teeth, so you knock out all of my teeth. If we continue to follow this line of behavior, then all of us will end up eyeless, limbless, toothless and *truth*-less. To be non-violent is to consider the rights of another. The general well-being of humanity and the world – "*jagatah sthiti karanam*" ought to be a critical consideration in calibrating and carrying out our responses.

Dharma means understanding of one's talents and needs and being sensitive to others' needs and talents. In my pursuit to express my talents and fulfill my needs, I should learn to cooperate with others, because they also have the same right! Others are also children of God. We all have our needs to fulfill. One should not assert, "I alone need fulfillment," and neglect others' needs and fulfillment. People are uncomfortable with a person who has such a dictatorial attitude. Everyone will oppose him or her. Even though you may be very talented, skilled and articulate, people will secretly hate you and try to undermine your projects. Like what happened to Winston Churchill: thousands came to hear him during election rallies. But when the votes were counted, Churchill lost the election, that, too, after leading the country to victory in the Second World War! People had a secret dislike for him due to his relentless, ruthless, self-promotion. Others may not have your talents, but they have their own.

Allowing Space for Others

During my public lecture tours, often there are two or three people wanting to sing. Different people have different talents, but one person tries to dominate the whole show, shutting out everyone else. He enjoys a natural, historical advantage and overpowers others. His talent may be greater, but others deserve a chance to discover *their* talents. The audience may enjoy one person's singing more, but if the other people who are talented are not given an opportunity, such an individual will create ill will in the whole environment. When the time comes, such a person is voted out.

Similarly, Margaret Thatcher was a highly efficient woman, but her own ministers turned against her. Such a thing can happen when you fail to give others opportunity to explore and develop. One can move furniture around, place it in a corner and expect it to stay put until you come back, because furniture is a thing without its own needs. But individuals have unique needs, and you cannot treat them like furniture. Therefore, in my pursuit to discover my niche in this complex world, and discover my *dharma* – that is, to match my talents with my needs – I also have to be sensitive to the needs and talents of others.

Existence Means Co-Existence

Bio-diversity is necessary for survival of individual life forms. To promote and accept diversity in the cultural context means being considerate of another person's needs. If someone serves your purpose, it is your duty to serve his or her purpose, also. Together we have to challenge each other, serve each other, and be sensitive to each other's needs. These are very important values. The ability to restrain impulses is an essential component of *dharma*, which again is a critical survival skill. Sensitivity to others and our willingness to integrate his or her needs in our projects is what we call "emotional intelligence" or soft skills.

Normally, when we first meet another person, our inner reaction is fear. Though he may or may not be talented – the very presence of other person creates fear: "He may take away whatever I have. He may outshine me. His popularity and success may threaten my own popularity and success." Through such thoughts, we accumulate anger, fear, jealousy, anxiety and tension, and relate with others on the basis of our imaginary fears and past conditioning. Because we have no practice of restraining our emotions, our normal social discourse is vitiated by these kinds of private fears. We have not developed the social and soft skills to interact with other people. But ultimately we must, for our own benefit, because no individual exists in a vacuum.

To fulfill our needs, we must maneuver in a complex system. If you live on an island all alone, what will you do? You will spend your whole life catching fish and eating them raw. Living all alone one cannot fulfill or explore one's innate potential. Others are necessary. Each individual brings his or her uniqueness to situations and circumstances. One prepares food, another brings water, a third makes clothing, and another looks idle but generates all kinds of discoveries.

Every plant, every person, every situation or relationship is unique. When we accept and promote diversity, every individual can explore and express himself and gain his own unique satisfaction. Satisfaction cannot be standardized. Once we accept that, we become more sensitive to the other person's needs – and that raises your consciousness to a higher level.

When we help others grow, others happily help your growth. This is the meaning of a civil society. If all the fingers are together, you have a fist that has a punch. If the fingers are separate, anyone can overpower you. As the saying goes, "If we don't hang together we will be hung separately!" That kind of synergy and sensitivity is to be cultivated.

Spiritual Satisfaction and Material Affluence

What is ultimately beneficial is that which gives us a sense of well-being. There are no external standards for that. You cannot use a thermometer to measure the degree of your contentment and satisfaction. Even though you are my son, I cannot decide what determines your sense of well-being. I cannot say what gives you inner contentment. As far as deep satisfaction is concerned, each individual has to decide for himself. You provide your own internal standard. Ultimately, you must decide what is good for you.

You may initially be ready to sacrifice some of your immediate needs in anticipation of greater good in the future, but you must see the light at the end of the tunnel. At the end of the day you must feel that something good is happening to you or for you. If that does not happen you will refuse to cooperate with others and, as a consequence, others will not cooperate with you and may even become your enemies. Then, instead of fulfilling your needs, you will waste your life fighting with those enemies.

Similarly, you may have all the external, material comforts and still you will feel no deep sense of satisfaction – you will be comfortably unhappy! That is another paradox under which we live. All the comforts abound – air-conditioning, a refrigerator, carpets, televisions, computers, pillows and a good bed. Sitting comfortably in your air-conditioned living room, you watch the news on television. You need not even move from your chair, using the channel changer to flip from station to station. You can raise or lower the room temperature several degrees, add another pillow behind your back, snack on potato chips – but still you are unhappy. For lasting happiness you need to know who you are. The issue involves your spiritual well-being, your need to unfold and express yourself.

It is your responsibility to know who you are, in the deeper sense of that phrase. We require a certain amount of affluence because, without it, we cannot think of the Spirit. If I were to ask you to meditate on the *Brahman* in the mid-summer heat of the Rajasthan desert without the benefit of a fan, with flies and mosquitoes buzzing around your head, could you meditate on *Brahman*? Try it. It's impossible. Sankara advises "*praninam abhyudaya nishreyas hetuh*" – we require certain "material comfort for spiritual well-being."

Exploring the Dimensions of Dharma

Our wisdom tradition shows us many dimensions and offers multiple definitions of *dharma*. One is *svabhavo dharma* – *dharma* is that which refers to your innate nature or *prakriti*. Whatever your nature is, that is your *dharma* – your natural expression. Honestly following that nature is your *dharma*. The *Gita* says, "*Sreyan sva-dharmo vigunah para dharmat svanusthitat / svabhava-niyatam karma kurvan n'apnoti kilbisam*". "One's own duty, in congruence with one's nature (even if inferior when compared to another) is more meritorious than the apparently well-performed duty which imitates another. For no sin is incurred by one doing works ordained according to one's nature" (18:47). If you go against your *svabhava* you create conflict. *Svabhava niyatam karma* – "Our *karmas*, our responses, should be determined by our *svabhava* or 'our nature'." But that idea mistakenly fosters a passive sense about the meaning of *dharma*: you just move according to your *svabhava* and don't make any effort, like a log of wood floating down a river. Wherever the river goes, you go. Passivity defines animals' instinctive behavior rather than that of humans. An animal behaves according to its *svabhava* because it is *un*conscious of its potential.

There is a story about the *sannyasi*, who, while taking a bath in the river, tried to save a drowning scorpion by picking him up. Whenever the *sannyasi* lifted the scorpion from the water, it stung him, and the *sannyasi* would quickly drop it. Then again he lifted the scorpion, trying to save it. Again the scorpion stung him. Again he would drop it, and pick it up. Again it stung him. Then, finally, someone interrupted this routine by asking, "Swamiji, why this circus? You keep protecting that scorpion, and every time you save him, he stings you!" The *sannyasi* replied, "My *dharma* is to save the scorpion. It is the scorpion's *dharma* to sting me. I follow my *dharma*, and the scorpion follows its *dharma*. If I try to kill that scorpion, then I will be following the *dharma* of the scorpion. There are many such scorpions in this world. I don't want to add to their population. I persist in my *dharma* and watch the scorpion following his." The *sannyasi* taught the valuable lesson in *dharma* – that each creature follows its inborn nature or *dharma* uninfluenced by others' *dharma*.

Nivriti and Pravriti Dharma

In the introduction to his Commentary on the *Bhagavad Gita*, Sankara defines *dharma* as, "*Dhividho hi vedokto dharma pravrti lakshano nivrti lakshana ca*". There are two paths of *dharma*. One path is *pravriti* and the other is *nivriti*. Those who are extroverted and inclined towards outer pursuits follow *pravriti marga*. Others who are introverted and attracted to inner pursuits follow *nivriti marga*. For the animal kingdom, there is only exploration of the outer world. Animals don't explore a world of inner dimensions, creating knowledge systems like psychology, philosophy and religion.

According to these two general divisions of *dharma* – the outer and inner pursuits – there are two disciplines: one path of discipline is for the householder and the other for the *sannyasin*. The active path explores the outer world and gives less attention to inner exploration. And, although, the *sannyasi* may be active in the world, his life is dedicated to inner exploration.

Active and Passive Dharma

The individual who defines *dharma* passively is akin to Sita, who accepted her life circumstances – her life in exile from her husband, Rama – as fated, *vidhi*. She endured her ordeal with a calm, stoic disposition, thinking it her duty as a wife.

The passive definition accepts: "This is my *dharma* or duty; this is my nature and I follow along accordingly." A passive definition of *dharma* is to simply "do as your nature dictates or your duty demands." Some people say, "Swamiji, everything is determined by *Bhagavan* (God). Whatever He has ordained for me, I accept. That's why I sit here like a stone. Let the Lord make whatever he wants of me." That is a very passive way of understanding God's mission and purpose for you and *not* a proper understanding of *dharma*.

The passive sense of *dharma* is more applicable to animals than to human life. All animals behave according to their nature. All cows are vegetarian and cannot exercise their will to become non-vegetarian. Their *dharma* is passive. When you say "*svabhava niyatam karma*," that definition is passive. However, humankind is of a different nature than the animal, and *svabhava* is to be defined in an active way.

One who defines *dharma* in an active sense insists upon developing their individual potential through dynamic interaction with their environment. Lord Krishna or Mahatma Gandhi are pre-eminent examples of active *dharma*. According to the principle of active *dharma*, one's character develops through moral, spiritual and intellectual disciplines. Such an individual cultivates virtues consciously, in an effort to discover the limits of his abilities, while interacting with the world.

Dharma is to be defined in this active sense. Unlike animals, we human beings have a sense of self-awareness – we can dream and think of our own potentialities. If our human potential does not unfold, we feel dissatisfied. Therefore the human being requires the opportunity to unfold – and, for that, disciplines are necessary.

You are a partner in God's creation. God says, "Be yourself; don't be an imitation of others." You are an individual; you are unique. We waste our whole life in imitation. Today we find teenagers with gray beards, imitating the 60-year-old, famous Indian actor, Amitabh Bacchan. In America teenagers imitate rock stars. What a confusion in the imitator's mind – and for *our* minds as well! We are unable to interpret what we see: the person before us looks 16, but his beard suggests that he is 60 years old! The effort to become like another reduces your individuality to a level of foolishness. God has given you individuality.

Action, according to the *Law of Dharma* promotes the well-being of all and nourishes the uniqueness of individuals. We want to be unique persons, don't we? We want to contribute something to the orchestra of the world, to the garden of the universe. We want to be a unique flower. This garden, of course, has many flowers and the whole garden is situated in a highly complex system of biodiversity. All these facets are important – biodiversity, the variety of flowers and the fact that, in that glorious universe, you are a special flower.

Be dignified in your own way. Capture your own unique identity and dignity. Respect yourself, your uniqueness. Don't be blown about by the prevailing winds like a dried leaf. Take charge of your life.

Active Dharma and Self-Discipline

Active *dharma* is a set of values and virtues by which you discipline yourself. The active definition of *dharma* proposes that, in an effort to explore your potential, you will discipline yourself, and, in the process, help yourself and others grow, individually and jointly.

Dharma means certain virtues that you adopt in life – a virtuous life, a proper and a righteous life. For that one has to restrain oneself. Why? So that you can develop your talents and have better relationships! You may have the talent, but to develop your talents, you need to apply purposeful effort. You cannot just sit idly and become a musician. Discipline becomes a very important aspect of *dharma*. Hence, *dharma* is defined as *achara prabhavo dharma* – "*dharma* is born of *achara*, self discipline or good conduct." One has to discipline oneself. You cannot discipline a lion beyond a limit. You cannot make a lion a vegetarian, because that would go against its nature. The lion follows its nature. But humans, being conscious of their potential, discipline themselves and can make choices for their betterment. That is the meaning of "self-consciousness." We all are self-conscious beings, but tables and rocks are not self-conscious. Unlike humans, the cow does not suffer the problem of its own uniqueness. Although the cow is a unique being, the cow is not conscious of itself.

Non-Violent Problem Solving

When you are conscious of yourself, you are also conscious of your potential, your needs. Unless that potential is developed, you will feel dissatisfied. That is why there is no dissatisfaction among animals, but the conscious human being is more often than not dissatisfied!

Never do you see two buffaloes sitting and discussing family problems! One buffalo cries, "My wife never listens to me." Then the other buffalo argues, "I think your wife is better. My wife beats me." Such discussions are never heard among animals. Only among human beings does this experience of dissatisfaction occur. We are dissatisfied because we are conscious of our potential.

I hear a frequent complaint that goes something like this: "Swamiji, at the office I don't feel any sense of satisfaction. My talents are not recognized. No one gives me the opportunity I deserve. Therefore, I am going to quit and join a music troupe. There, at least, they will recognize my talents." And it is true: you do have enormous talent; others do, too. But do you put in adequate effort? Capabilities flourish in the soil of sustained self-effort. We also need to be sensitive to another person's needs and synergize with their projects.

In an enlightened society – a society that is grounded in *dharma* – manipulative tactics will not work. Sri Vyasa says, "*Dharma* is that which is based on *achara*, good." If a particular act doesn't promote your well-being or reflect good conduct, that act is *adharma*. Good conduct is where you incorporate the interests of the other. That is called non-violence. In settling disputes some individuals take recourse to violence to fulfill their purposes. Because resources are limited, most disputes are resolved by means of violence.

Suppose your children don't listen to you, what do you do? You shout abusive words and then ask the child not to use such language. Is it any wonder the child will not listen? Verbal abuse and double standards are forms of violence that we exercise on our children. To paraphrase Mahatma Gandhi, if you want the child to change, you should become the change that you want to see in him. That is a non-violent way of engaging in a discussion and resolving conflict.

Dharma as Ahimsa and Satyam

There are two additional definitions of *dharma*. The first is, "*Satyameva jayate na'anrutam satyena pantha vitatha devayanah*". "*Dharma* is Truth; That alone prevails. The path to *dharma* is paved with Truth." (*Mundaka Upanishad* 3:2.5-6). The second is, "*Ahimsa paramo dharma,*" "Non-violence is supreme virtue or *dharma*." (*Mahabharta, anushasana parva*. 115:1) *Satyam* means we are honest with each other and with ourselves in expressing our deeper-most thoughts and needs. That attitude promotes the culture of dialogue and facilitates communication.

Ahimsa means dialoguing, on the basis of Truth, and deciding issues. This non-violent means of resolving conflict is possible when all of us express our needs, put them on the table and discuss. Otherwise we become violent and manipulative; we become dictators and hypocrites. *Ahimsa* requires patience – patience to explore solutions in a comprehensive manner. We develop complexes and neuroses because we are not honest in stating our needs and, then, as a consequence, we try to manipulate others. We don't have to manipulate others or become violent.

Have you noticed that while we are manipulating we always smile – a smile as false as the teeth behind it. For example, when you go door to door throughout the neighborhood seeking donations, one of your neighbors opens the door and sees you standing there with a crescent moon smile on your face. You smile and give a hearty, "Hello! I know you are a very kind and thoughtful neighbor, etc. etc." You continue trying to convince him – always with the same smile pasted on your face, with your sweet words and a lofty philosophy describing your mission – until finally you have to come to the point, saying, "We have this program to support our organization.

We are asking for a donation of $10." The $10 dollars is not for me, it is for a worthy cause, helping the needy. It's a wonderful thing for society. Please donate. God will bless you."

Then, that neighbor flatly says, "I am not going to give any donation." The moment you hear that, inside your mind, your whole energy turns. The whole manipulative facade changes. The same energy you were utilizing for a worthy cause becomes a poison in your system, and you start condemning your neighbor: "That man is a boor. I never liked him, anyway. He was always greedy. He should be shipped to Siberia!"

You uttered all these sweet words because you were trying to manipulate him, and then, when he rejected your proposition you abandoned your goodwill. Your dishonest smile became an honest scowl. Why don't you give him the dignity of being himself? He considered everything you said and decided that you don't deserve that donation, or that he can't afford to give the donation. It is his privilege to make that choice, and you have no business to condemn him for that. You must allow him that freedom of choice. That is non-violence. Once we understand the meaning of non-violence, then there is no ill will. But if you try to manipulate another person, even in a very nice way, your manipulative tactics will ultimately fall through. Instead of listening to all you were telling him about your wonderful project, he was thinking, "What's the catch? There is a string attached to this." You cannot fool people for long.

Whenever manipulative tactics don't work, we become angry, and anger fosters violence. We decide to settle issues by twisting the opponent's arm, and the problem is solved! A child in such circumstances will cringe, crawl away into a corner, crying, and then fall asleep. Your friends will simply run away. Whatever the case, by resorting to violence you lose the opportunity to incorporate the other into your schemes. *Dharma* means an ability to incorporate, to encompass or embrace the other, to be sensitive and respect the other person's individuality, respect his or her need to grow in his or her own way.

Ahimsa means, "*Loka samastha sukhinah bhavantu*," "Let all be happy. Let all develop their talents. Let all fulfill their needs. Let no one be denied their right." Together we all can have the opportunity to grow. We want everyone to contribute their efforts and to fulfill their needs because work gives us self-respect. It is not only your needs, but also your talents and your contributions that are important. If I deny you the right to contribute, then you will develop a sense of low self-esteem. Suppose I make an offer to you: "I'll give you three meals a day and a bed to sleep in, also, but, there is only one requirement: 'Don't do anything in return!'" Although you may think you are doing the other person a favor, that method is a very inhuman way of dealing with others. You deny them any opportunity to express *their* talents.

Understanding another person's uniqueness is an important component in understanding *dharma*. By understanding another's uniqueness, you understand your own uniqueness and needs. Only by promoting the other person's uniqueness can you discover your uniqueness. Otherwise both of you sink to a low level of dynamics. Even in a prison there is also discipline and equilibrium. But we can hardly appreciate the prison environment as source of *real* discipline. Discipline of this variety is imposed upon you rather than being born out of your self-understanding, satisfaction and self-imposed restraint. *Dharma* means to be sensitive to other persons, and for that we apply certain self-disciplines or restrictions upon our own behavior.

Putting it all together: from Ahimsa *to* Svadharma

Having thoroughly examined the dynamics of *dharma*, we are ready to understand its underlying philosophical basis. There are several dynamic levels in the operation of the *Law of Dharma*. Although the individual is unique, he is not an isolated person. That unique individual is situated in a psychological environment and in a socio-cultural context collectively known as *varnashrama*. Expression, conditioned by one's particular socio-cultural and individual circumstances, is known as *varnashrama dharma*.

Your unique individuality – your peculiar needs and talents – and your uniqueness flower in a socio-cultural milieu. You require expression for the development of your talents and satisfaction of your needs. Family, society and culture provide the platform for that. *Varnashrama dharma* is again grounded in what is called *Sanatana dharma*, Universal changeless values. *Sanatana dharma* refers to Universal Consciousness – that which supports socio-cultural systems and psychological environments, and serves as the ground for the individual and his creativity. Out of the sum total of individuals' collective interactions with the environment emerges the historical context of culture and psychology and, finally, a particular individual. The individual is the capstone of this creation, a pinnacle of this very complex process. As an individual your roots are in *Brahman*.

Sanatana dharma also means a universal and changeless values system that is applicable everywhere, what Aldous Huxley called "Perennial Wisdom." Everyone is to follow the ideal of Truth and practice *ahimsa* or non-violence. *Ahimsa* (non-violence) is the heart of *sanatana dharma*. The value of *ahimsa*, alone, will last in this world. Non-violence means respect for another's uniqueness. When you apply that law, others extend the same courtesy to you. You create an atmosphere where several flowers can bloom, and your garden will be marvelously colorful and diverse. A single flower is appreciated more in the context of the whole panorama! If I conquer you, manipulate or liquidate you, how *can I* survive? If there is only one flower we cannot call it a garden. In the process of eliminating you, I ensure my own annihilation. In a garden, the beauty is in the multitude of flowers, the array of colors, as well as in the individual flower.

The context for the individual flower is an environment of love, a mutual nourishing and cherishing environment of non-violence, an environment of growing together and discovering our destiny mutually, individually and collectively. Buddha's dictum is, "Life belongs to those who promote it, not to those who destroy it." When I promote you, you belong to me; and when you promote me, I belong to you. If I promote only myself at the cost of the other, then I am ensuring our mutual destruction. Such behavior is madness! But that is how we are primarily engaged with others: I destroy you; you destroy me. Conversely, when I promote the other, then I can expect the same courtesy in return.

Dharma is to be understood and applied contextually. Application depends upon one's occupation, age and placement in life. Based upon these considerations you calibrate your responses. The *Vedas* call this *svadharma* or individual *dharma*.

Ahimsa is to be applied in accordance with the situation. Sometimes you may be required to tell a lie for the well-being of society or for another's sake. The function of *ahimsa* may also depend upon your vocation. Suppose you are in the army and the enemy attacks. At that moment you cannot object, saying, "This is not my *dharma*. I am a votary of *ahimsa*." You must shoot back. For the sake of your life, as well as the lives of others, you have to preempt his attack and shoot. But that does not mean that one should make killing a habit! After 20 years of service in the armed forces, when you retire, you should not sit at home and cry, "Swamiji, nowadays there is nobody to shoot!" While you are in the army, shooting is appropriate and necessary. In another situation, however, to be ready to be killed rather than kill may be the appropriate response.

Apat Dharma – Contingency Responses

There are several factors involved in calibrating any given response. First is your occupation and station (*varna*) in life; secondly, your age (*ashrama*), then *desa* and *kala* (place and time), and, finally, *nimita* (the contingencies). Of these several coordinates of dharma, *nimita* or *apat dharma* is critical in determining your responses. This is *dharma* expected in the face of crises, when an unusual set of demands is imposed upon you. Within a given culture, there are general rules for *varnashrama dharma*, but sometimes, even in that given culture, those rules may have to change. This is referred to as "*apat dharma*."

Let me offer an example: Parasurama was a *Brahmin* whose *dharma* is to study, teach and propagate the *Vedas*. In his particular situation, Parasurama could not fulfill his *dharma* for a period of time, due to the corrupt state of the government. Thus, Parasurama took up an axe and went around fighting corruption. This period in Parasurama's life gives us an example of *apat dharma*.

Another example of *apat dharma* is from the life of Vishvamitra, the *Kshetriya* (warrior) who became a *Brahmin*. Vishvamitra was not supposed to eat meat – that, too, dog meat. Once, *Vishvamitra* was passing through in a drought-hit region where food was very scarce. He went hungry for days and was very thirsty. His morals were such that he did not eat dog meat, but one day met a *chandala*. [*Chandala* means "one who eats dog meat."] The *chandala* said, "Sir, I can give you some dog meat." Vishvamitra reflected, "Fine, I am hungry. At this moment my primary responsibility is to keep my body and soul together. The rest of my duties come later, because, if I don't eat, then I will starve to death and the study of the *Vedas* will cease and *dharma* will vanish. Self-preservation is primary. If I have to eat a cooked dog for that, I will." Then Vishvamitra replied, "Yes, whether it is cooked or not, I don't care. Please give me something to eat." And Vishvamitra ate dog meat along with the *chandala*. Afterwards the *chandala* said, "Oh, I didn't notice. I have some cooked grain, also. Can I give you some of that now?" Vishvamitra curtly replied, "No, I don't eat from *chandala's* house." The *chandala* was surprised, "You don't eat from a *chandala's* house? Just now you had a meal in my home, and that too, from my pot of dog meat!" But within a second the situation had radically changed, and Vishvamitra immediately reverted to his *Brahmanic* values. Subsequently, too, he refused the food served in the home of a lower caste individual.

When Vishvamitra was starving, he performed what is called a "contingency *dharma*," *apat dharma*. For his own survival – in that situation and at that moment – he had to adjust his values. Now circumstances had changed. This expertise, this nimble-footedness is important in applying *dharma*. *Dharma* protects those who follow the path of *dharma*: "*Dharmo rakshati rakshitah*." Sage Manu says quite unequivocally: "*Dharma* itself protects those who follow the path of *dharma*" (*Manu Smriti*. 8:15).

Dynamic Dharma

These, then, are three determinants of individual *dharma*, personal responses to situations – *Sanatana dharma*, *varnashrama dharma*, and *apat dharma*. When all these various aspects of *dharma* are understood, you will know what exactly your response ought to be in any given situation. The whole thing is calibrated in your contemplative consciousness, as you interact with the world. You design your responses to this ever-changing situation according to your needs and talents as an individual.

Dharma is a very dynamic concept. Individual uniqueness

is its central tenet. When you weave your understanding of *dharma* around this understanding, you will be able to simultaneously act as an individual, as a social being and as a spiritual person and promote personal and communal well-being. If you miss any of these facets of the various "levels" of *dharma*, you will be harming yourself, either psychologically, socially or spiritually. You will not enjoy your individuality, uniqueness and happiness. Some people lead a thwarted, depressed, meaningless, miserable hypocritical life, in the name of spirituality, thinking that they are following *dharma*. They feel hindered, hampered and unable to unfold. That is not spirituality. Spirituality is when you and others grow, touch the Spirit, and realize your dreams in the process. If you are not growing, if you continuously sacrifice or become a sacrificial goat (*devanam pashuh*), you are a foolish, *adharmic* person. You may be good, but you will be good for nothing! As a consequence of the interactive life process, everyone should grow.

This duty is a very complex process. It is not as simple as being told what to do. You are a unique individual; who knows your inner fire better than you? No one can decide what is best for you in a given situation. However, I can tell you what the requirements are for *svadharma* or *mama-dharma* ("my duty"), but it is your own very deep hunger that drives you. You alone know that.

How do you mix and moderate all these factors of *dharma*

and make the right decision at the right time? It is, indeed, a matter of personal vigilance and divine blessing. Sri Vyasa says, "*Dharmasya prabhu achyutah*," meaning, "God is the inspiration for *Dharma*." The ability to calibrate the right response, at any given moment, is a blessing from God.

Understanding all this, it is your responsibility to design your responses to the ever-changing situations in this world. In that process, you will activate your inner powers, your inner Self. This is your responsibility; this is your freedom and moment of Truth.

Four

The Spiritual Law of Karma

Moral Cause and Consequences

The fourth law, the *Law of Karma*, is a very misunderstood, misconstrued and misapplied law. *Karma* has become a big hat that can be worn by anybody and has, therefore, lost its character. These days, you can explain anything by citing *karma*. If you are a very successful CEO, people say, "That's his *karma*." If you are an unemployed loafer, you will also hear, "That's your *karma*." No matter what, we bring *karma* as an explanation – and a theory that explains everything explains nothing! It is only a convenient means of escapism. *Karma* requires deeper examination.

Vedanta introduces the *Law of Karma* to explain experience. Most people use *karma* to explain their misfortunes. Suppose you fell from a tree and fractured your leg. You sigh in exasperation, "What can I do?" and add with despair and resignation, "It's my *karma*." Someone else wins a 30 million dollar lottery; his friends shake their heads in awe, "It must be his *karma*." We have no other way of explaining events.

If something negative happens, then it's one's *bad karma*; if something good happens, then it's one's *good karma*. In general, we use that word to explain an event or an experience which has already taken place. These uses give us an incomplete understanding and application of the *Law* of *Karma*.

The Ramayana's Conceptualization of Karma

Let us survey the use of *karma* in the literature of our Hindu wisdom tradition. In the *Ramayana*, Sita was abducted by Ravana and taken to Lanka. Sitting under the *shimshibah* in the *ashoka* forest, Sita heaved and sighed. In between her fits of emotion, she cried, "This is my *vidhi*. Inspite of my marriage to Rama, the great, valorous and all-powerful prince, and in spite of Rama's ability to single-handed defeat an army of 14,000 soldiers strong, he is unable to help me...and I am loyal to my husband. If I were disloyal then these things are understandable. Still this has happened to me. How can I explain it? This is my *vidhi*, my fate." That is what Sita cried as she sat in Ravana's garden.

Later, under the pretext of sending Sita to an *ashram*, Rama again banished her to the forest – no doubt, due to some talk show host, who, for the sake of gaining popularity, questioned her chastity! When this news reached Rama, he declared, "I again renounce Sita," and the pregnant Sita was again sent to the forest. When Sita realized that Lord Rama had abandoned her for the second time, she could only heave more sighs, and in between her sighs admit, "This is my *vidhi*. There is no other explanation."

The word "*vidhi*," here, means the same as "*karma*." Sita said, "I am fated to fall into such situations. No one, not even Lord Rama, can protect me." Rama himself is the Lord, yet he could not help her. Thus, Sita did not even use the word "providential," meaning, "This is God's will." As in Sita's story, *karma* is sometimes interpreted as *vidhi*. Some super-power, the *vidhi*, arbitrarily superintends the destiny of an individual life. We are all caught up in the clutches of that *vidhi*. We are little pawns in *vidhi's* hands. *Vidhi* precedes you wherever you go. This word, "*vidhi*," found in the *Ramayana* offers us only one limited explanation for inexplicable circumstances. There are other explanations of *karma*.

Karma *as a Retrospective Tool*

Karma theory is most often also used as a retrospective tool, to help understand what may have happened in the past and the present consequences. We use the *karma theory* to peer into the past for the sake of understanding our present condition. For example, if you had a trauma and were to see a psychologist, he may put you under hypnosis and conduct an age-regression session, taking you into your deep, hidden past, trying to discover psychological reasons for your problem. But that also is only a partial approach, and such practices may even create additional problems for you!

Everyone wants to know their past – but knowing it may be a very dangerous proposition! You discover that, in a past life, you were a rat, and your husband was a cat – natural enemies. You realize that even now you are natural enemies, but at least, as humans, you have some values to soften your relationship.

Now that you know who you both were, your situation is worse! Since *karma* theory supports the notion that once you were cat-rat personalities, you now bring these "past" memories into the present and develop multiple personalities or even schizophrenia. When you look at your husband's face, you see a rat with whiskers!

In actuality, the human personality is so complicated, with multiple layers of memory, that it is very difficult to determine what specific or multiple past experiences have been reactivated in your present circumstances.

Neither do you know what the future will bring. Your poking into previous lives and *karmas* only confuses your database and makes it more complicated for you to process information and predict the future. The whole problem becomes more and more murky. Therefore, God very wisely placed curtains between the past and present – like a drama performed on the stage of the theatre. What if someone accidentally pulled down the curtain between the front and back stage? The drama would cease to have its effect. The curtains must be in place in order to create a storyline and the effect of episodic movement. Then the drama becomes very meaningful.

Understand that you don't have to literally go back in time, or undergo age regression, in order to know your past. Your past is very much evident in your immediate circumstances. Whatever you are today is a continuation of your past. Nobody has to tell you that. The very quality and conditions of your present life are indicative of your past life.

The Mahabharata's Treatment of Karma *Theory*

Another application of *karma* theory, and a new development, appears in the *Mahabharata*. *Karma* is applied in the *Mahabharata* as a prognostic tool which is used to get insight into what will happen in the future. Whatever you are today, you will repeat in the future. The *Mahabharata* exploits this aspect of *karma*.

For example, for his father's sake, Bhishma took this great vow of *brahmacharya* (life long celibacy) known as Bhishma *pratijna*. This made Bhishma a king-maker, because he himself had no desire to become king. He was the wisest man in the Kuru kingdom; Vichitravirya and Chitrangada, his half-brothers and inheritors to the throne, were mediocre people. When Bhishma took this vow, the whole universe shook with the might of Bhishma's resolve. But then, life situations put pressure on this resolution. Because of this resolve, Bhishma could not become king and obtain his rightful place in the history and human affairs in Bharat. In his place he made Vichitravirya the king and Chitrangada as the heir-apparent. Furthermore, he was responsible for finding wives for his two brothers. Poor Bhishma! He must have been 92 years old at that time. He was such a tall, handsome, wiry man that any girl would fall in love with him. But due to his vow not to marry he didn't want to look at women.

In search of wives for his half-brothers, Bhishma went to Kashi where there were three young princesses seeking husbands. In those days, by your valorous deeds, you could woo a young woman who would then choose to become your wife. This process was called *svayamvara* – women choosing tournament winners as their husbands. Because of his vow not to marry, Bhishma was very afraid of engaging in the event. Many others kings came to the *svayamvara* to obtain the hands of the King of Kashi's three daughters, Amba, Ambalika, and Ambika. The king's daughters were paraded around, and a championship tournament was held. The three princesses were to select the most valorous men as their husbands, and would then be taken away by their suitors to their respective kingdoms.

Bhishma easily defeated all the other contestants and all three royal daughters quickly fell in love with him. Only with much difficulty could he convince two of the daughters that he had actually won them on behalf of his two half-brothers. When the daughters came to the Kuru kingdom, they found these two men were very weak and impotent but accepted the agreement anyway. However, the first daughter, Amba, declared, "Nothing doing, Bhishma. I will only marry you."

Now, Bhishma was in real trouble; to spurn the desire of a woman is to invite her eternal wrath. Poor Bhishma! Had he only anticipated the potential outcome of his vow not to marry, he may have saved himself so much trouble!

Amba's Revenge

If you hurt and humiliate a woman by spurning her advances, you will be consumed by her unquenchable fury. She can finish you off. Amba insisted that she would marry only Bhishma. Once a girl decides to marry you, there is no escape! She has enormous power to spread her net. Wherever you go, she will trail you and force you to fall into her trap! That is the strength of a woman's determination. Amba issued this ultimatum, "Either I marry you, or I will destroy you!"

Unable to persuade Bhishma to break his vow, Amba finally went to Parasurama, the *guru* of Bhishma. Parasurama, as Bhishma's *guru*, was the only person who could persuade Bhishma that this was the correct thing to do. Parasurama assured Amba, "Yes, you are right. Bhishma should marry you because he won you in the contest." Then Parasurama called

Bhishma and told him that he must marry Amba. Bhishma pleaded, "Sir, you are my *guru* and you taught me that one must be honest and honor one's word. I cannot break my vow and marry this girl."

Parasurama fought with him, but Bhishma was firm in his resolve and defeated Parasurama. Amba had nowhere to go, so in the fire of her fury she underwent self-immolation, all the while with this thought firmly in mind: "I will take another birth in which I will finish off this old man along with his vow!"

This story continued when Drupada, the King of Panchala, performed a *yajna*, and from that *yajna* fire three luminous offspring were born, Dristadyumna, Draupadi and Sikhandi. No one has as yet been able to determine if Sikhandi was born a girl or boy, but Drupada brought the child up as a boy. Nevertheless, Sikhandi was the *avatar*, the manifestation of Amba's thought and determination.

Just see the connections! When Bhishma was fighting with Arjuna in the decisive battle of the *Mahabharata*, Sikhandi appeared on Arjuna's side. Sikhandi was a sibling of Draupadi, and Draupadi was married to Arjuna – how the *karma* network orchestrates events and creates future effects! It is difficult to follow all this, the labyrinthine *karmic* networking described in the *Mahabharata*! "*Gahana karmano gatih*" (4:17). "Mysterious are the ways of *karma*" laments Krishna in the *Bhagavad Gita*.

Finally, confronting Sikhandi in battle, Bhishma just gave up in disgust. He had such a great respect for women that he could not fight with someone whom he even *thought* might be a woman! Sikhandi accomplished her revenge, as a consequence. Bhishma was struck down and killed. Bhishma's inflexible adherence to his vow was ultimately responsible for his demise.

From this illustration we understand how one's past projects as the future, and that *karma* is both prospective and retrospective. This is the *Mahabarata's* treatment of *karma*, which goes beyond the concept of *vidhi* or fate in the *Ramayana*. In the *Ramayana*, you find a simple application of *karma* in terms of fate and predetermination, about which you can do nothing. Akin to this general understanding of fate, *karma* is also used as a tool, a tool which explains your present situation or circumstances. But in *Mahabarata, karma* acquires a very complex treatment and is used to explain future events.

Karma *in Yoga Vasistha*

There is another literature called the *Yoga Vasistha* which is a compendium of Sage Vasistha's advice to Rama. There the treatment of *karma* is totally different. In *Yoga Vasistha, karma* means "freedom of choice." You have the freedom to choose your actions, and you must exercise that choice. In a telling example, *Yoga Vasistha* simply notes, "The *supta simha* (a sleeping lion) will not get its prey!" As the story goes, a lion lies down and imagines, "If I am to eat, food will come to me and jump right into my mouth." Most of us think like that: "If I am to receive something, it will come my way. Otherwise I'm not fated to get it." *Yoga Vasistha* refutes this conceptualization in a very contemptuous way. If you think like the lazy lion – that you don't even have to open your mouth – then nothing will happen and, slowly, you will starve to death!

The lion should remain alert and vigilant, like a calm pool of energy, noiselessly watching and ever-ready to spring into action. When a deer or prey runs across its path, the lion assesses the direction of the wind, calculates the speed and distance of the prey. With all his muscles tense in preparation for the chase, the lion finally springs into action and snatches its prey. The lion enjoys munching and gnawing for some time and finally swallows and digests the flesh. Then only can a lion survive.

All this predatory activity requires vigilance. Even with the slightest mistake, the lion will fail to catch its prey. If the lion sleeps, thinking that *vidhi* will bring food, it will soon die. The sprit of *Yoga Vasistha* propounds a philosophy of pro-activity and declares that you must take charge of your life!

Understanding Karma's *Complexity*

When we explain *Karma* theory we need to do so holistically, incorporating these three ideas from the *Ramayana*, the *Mahabharata* and the *Yoga Vasistha*. The *Law of Karma* declares, "You are a free, choice-making agent; every action is a moral choice and invariably produces a corresponding result."

In the previous chapter on *Dharma*, we discussed your unique personhood. Being a unique individual, you act as an independent center of value and initiative that makes choices. Of course, you must consider everything, the totality of the situation – processing all available information, keeping all possible outcomes in mind, and choosing a line of action. Once you make a choice, you are responsible for your actions. This is what makes you an independent person rather than a puppet manipulated by someone else.

Most of the time, we blame others for our misfortune. Suppose you are not doing well in life; the first people you criticize will be your very own parents: "Because of my parents I am a failure." Alternately, you think of psychological explanations: "When I was a baby my mother didn't put me in her lap, kiss and cuddle me. I was deprived of that maternal love; so, now I suffer from low self-esteem."

In America, children even file suits against their parents! For your stupidity in making choices, your parents are taken to court! How long will you remain with that kind of escapist, victim attitude? If you blame *your* parents, they ought to also blame *their* parents. Where will the lawsuits end? All of us will end up in court! Lawyers will be happy. When are you going to take charge of your life?

If not your parents, then the government is to blame: "Because of that Nehruvian policy I am doing poorly in business." What is the connection between Nehruvian policy and your inefficiency? Ultimately you blame your stars. "My *sani* (Saturn) is not placed well, and that is why I have a difficult life. Whatever I undertake becomes a colossal failure." Why? "Sani is the mischief-maker." What about *your* responsibility? Poor *sani* is struggling to find its place somewhere in the heavenly firmament. The Sun's gravity is pulling it one way, and other planets are exerting their force another direction, and you are blaming that *sani* for your misfortunes? God has made you a responsible person. You alone are responsible for your failure!

We cannot blame anybody for whatever we are. We must have the courage and heroism to accept the fact that we are squarely and singularly responsible for whatever we have made and whatever we make of our lives. The *Law of Karma* says: "You are an independent center of value creation and choice making is your responsibility."

The *Shastras* put it this way: "*Karthum sakyam, akarthum sakyam, anyatha va karthum sakyam.*" "You can act in many possible ways. Do, don't do, postpone or do differently." These are the possibilities. You can reach a theatre by car, by riding a bicycle, walking or getting a ride from your neighbor, or you can decide not to go at all! It is your choice. Most people postpone decisions and actions, but postponement is also a decision! At one time or another we have all probably failed to return a borrowed book or to repay a loan from a friend. "Tomorrow I'll return it," or "Tomorrow I'll pay you back," you retort. Everyone procrastinates.

Karma *and Individual Responsibility*

The *Law of Karma* affirms, "As an independent individual, you make your own choices." That is the meaning of individuality, responsibility and independence. You are indivisible, whole and valuable in yourself. You are not an object in the hands of others. As an individual person, you are a source and judge of values. Ultimately, you have to reflect, check within yourself, "Does the choice I am making contribute to my well-being?"

Ordinarily, *karma* is understood in a passive manner, but we must explore all the three meanings of *karma*. *Karma* gives us an understanding of the past as well as the future, empowers us to take charge of our present life and fashion it according to our dreams. Your destiny is determined by your deeds and your deeds by your choices. The *Law of Karma* says, "*You are the creator of your destiny*," a definition that we have totally misunderstood!

Karma *and* Karmaphala

If this is the general understanding of the *Law of Karma*, then let us try to see its various nuances, implications and applications. There are two words that have become very popular in the world – *yoga* and *karma*. Everybody is "doing" *yoga* and talking about their good and bad *karma*. All over the world people have accepted these two words as a part of their daily language.

Yoga derives from the root "*yug*," and means "that which unites." *Dharma* is derived from "*dharyate*" and means "that which supports." What exactly does *karma* mean? *Karma* comes from the Sanskrit root "*kr – kriyate iti karma.*" "*Kriyate*" is "to act; a new impulse introduced into the present scheme of things." The *Gita* defines *karma* as, "*Bhuta-bhavodbhava-karo visargah karma samjnitah*" "*Karma* is creative activity which projects the world of beings and things" (8:3). *Karma* is a new energy or independent impulse introduced by an individual into the orchestra of events.

Karma means action and not a *re*-action. *Karma* is not repetition but new energy and a new initiative. Any *karma* creates *phala*, its fruit or result. *Karma* and *phala* are one continuum.

When you put money in the bank, the story isn't over. You make note of that in your savings book. You check the periodicity of the interest payment, and at the end of the quarter, you see how much interest has been accumulated. Then you estimate your interest over the next three years, and see that you have 100,000 *rupees* with 10 % interest! That is the *phala*; what you invest now grows and produces a result. A particular act does not stand independently, but any action creates ripples and effects. Finally, these ripples culminate and bear the fruit of your actions.

The Cause and Consequence Continuum

When you say *karma*, it signifies *both* the cause and the consequence – *karma* and *phala*. The word *karma* signifies not only an action, a new impulse, the new energy poured into the scheme of things, but it also signifies the consequences. When you put your savings in a bank, it is *karma*, an action. When you get the interest, you then say, "That's my good *karma*." If you won the lottery, and instead of saving your prize money, you spend it all foolishly, you will soon have nothing left. Then you are apt to whine, "Well, it's my bad *karma*! I'm even worse off than before I won the lottery!" Don't simply say it is your *karma*. Rather, realize your loss is a result of the deeds your have done.

Action and consequence are a continuum – not a single event, but a series of events culminating in a definite result. Our first understanding ought to be that the *Law of Karma* includes both an action *and* its consequence.

The second implication of this law is that the cause and consequence are not unrelated but are a related phenomena. The consequence or result is the modified cause. The Indian logic is, "*karya karanayoh abheda*," that there is "no difference between the *karana* (cause) and the *karya* (effect)." Your action and the result are not different energies; they are identical. You cannot say the effect has nothing to do with the cause; nor can you say that cause has nothing to do with effect. In fact, the effect is the cause modified in time. If you make a pot out of clay, what is the pot but an effect of the clay modified in time. Time is the only intervention; otherwise both cause and effect are the same.

When your son becomes 55, he will look exactly like his father at that age, because the effect is the modified cause. If you do a deed, the result will be determined by the quality and property of the deed. For example, if I smile and give you flowers, what will you do? You are unlikely to frown at me and say, "How dare you give me flowers?" A sensible person will smile and graciously receive the gift. When I am kind to you, you return kindness. The result is determined by the cause. The result is nothing but the cause modified in time.

You can witness the cause and effect continuum. I am sure if I smile, you will smile back, unless you are drunk or have something to hide! Once it happened that we went to see a holy place. We were anticipating seeing it, so we were very happy and smiling. But when someone greeted us at the gate with a frown and grumbled, "You can't just walk in here!" We were wondering, "What is the matter with him?" Then they gave us visitor name tags and called two people to escort us around the complex, as if we needed guards. Contrary to this experience, people are generally welcoming. When you smile – even at a stranger – you will receive a smile in return. The cause modified gives the effect.

The Human Animal

The third principle of *karma* is that "*every action is a moral choice.*" Action is *not* a moral choice for an animal. An animal acts instinctually and impulsively, whereas, when humans act, they make moral choices. When a lion kills a deer, we don't blame the lion for what it has done, because it is its nature to hunt and kill its prey. By appeasing its hunger the lion is fulfilling its *dharma*, preserving itself. A satiated lion doesn't continue hunting. It falls asleep. After you and I have a good meal, we begin the hunt! We start thinking about how to cheat somebody or how to make more money by some nefarious means. After our hunger is appeased, all our problems begin. Although the lion cannot engage in an immoral act or an unethical act, we humans can and do!

Our every action constitutes a moral choice, for two reasons: First of all, we judge our actions by the consequences they create. A lion will not judge its actions. Suppose the lion falls into a ditch and is in agonizing pain. The lion won't think, "I should not have fallen into the ditch! It's only because I was careless that this happened." The lion experiences pain, but it does not bring past memories to bear on the incident and then psychoanalyze and judge. Whereas, we humans gaze retrospectively, analyze our deeds and judge our actions in terms of the result they engender.

The second reason why *rishis* say every action is a moral choice is because every action is performed by an intender. Or we can say that there is an intention behind every action. Even reading this book is with intention. The intention could be as innocuous as this, "I'll quickly fall sleep, and without even having to take my sleeping pills!" Or you may enjoy spending your time reading, having nothing else to do at home. Or perhaps there are no other options at that time. Every action is intentional, goal-directed energy. No human being undertakes any action without an intention. Sankara says, "*Mudhobhi phalam anudhisya karma na kurute,*" "Not even a fool will undertake an action without intention." The person behind every action expects a definite result. With that intention in mind he undertakes a specific action that he thinks will produce the desired result.

No Running Away

The fourth aspect of the *Law of Karma* is that the result of any action will finally visit the intender. If I undertake an action with an intention, where will the result finally collapse and abide? The action completes a loop when the result visits the intender!

Let me illustrate with a story. Valmiki was a thief who later reformed and wrote the *Ramayana*. A sage asked him this very question: "My dear son, first of all, do you know that you are doing something wrong? Do you know who will suffer the consequences of what you are doing?" Valmiki responded, "My family will! Because whatever I steal, I give to them." The sage replied, "No. Neither your wife nor your children will suffer the results. Finally, your negative actions will come and revisit you!"

Action produces a boomerang effect, and the intender becomes the final target of his or her own actions. No one can escape. Whatever action you initiate in this world may go a long way, but finally the action will find you out! You may have committed a murder and then escaped to Kashi where no one knew you. Then you shaved your head and, out of fear and guilt, became a *sannyasi*. At that time you were lean and skinny. Now you are plump and have grown a long beard and are sitting on the dais giving a discourse on *dharma*. While speaking, you suddenly smile, and someone in the audience recognizes you. He jumps up and shouts, "The *swami* sitting there is a murderer!" and you are caught!

A similar story is found in the Hindu *Puranas*. Once, it so happened, when the *asuras* and *devas* joined hands in churning the milky ocean, *amrit*, the nectar of immortality, was produced. Then the *asuras* ran away with the pot of nectar. Then Vishnu took the form of a woman and outwitted the *asuras*, running away with the pot of nectar. He went to *svargaloka* and began distributing the nectar to the *devas*. Then the *asuras* sent one representative *asura* in the disguise of a *brahmachari* to *svargaloka*. The *asura* slipped by the gatekeepers, *Surya* and *Chandra*. In the guise of a *brahmachari*, the *asura*, also received some *amrit* and drank it. Up to that time no one recognized who he was. When he imbibed the *amrit*, he was so gleeful that he laughed and accidentally bared his canine teeth. Sometimes, in glee your mask falls off. Immediately, *Surya* and *Chandra* charged with their swords and cut him into two. The two *asuras* became *rahu* and *ketu*.

Correspondingly, a time will come when the arm of *karma* will catch you. You may run away from whatever you have done, but the more you run away the more you run into the jaws of *karma*. As far as the *Law of Karma* is concerned, you will get the result of your actions. No one else will. Don't think, "I have nothing to do with my *karma*. I have become a *sannyasi*." Of course, if you are a *sannyasi* you can say, "*Karma* doesn't affect me; it only affects my body. My mind and body did it, but it does not affect *me*!" That's a different story; there is a "loop hole" for a *sannyasi*. But let's analyze that special circumstance.

If you are authentic in your *sannyasa* you remain unaffected whether you are tortured or in jail. "*Chidanandarupa shivoham, shivoham,*" "I am the ocean of Consciousness and Bliss." If you have the courage and the clarity and depth of vision to say and mean that great understanding, then you are a real *sannyasi*. Then alone are you skilled at using *karma* to reinvent yourself, because every experience becomes an opportunity to transcend!

Now, if all these aspects of the *Law of Karma* and its various dimensions are understood, then how do we apply the law?

What we Cannot Change

Every moment something happens to you; it can be either good or bad. Let us say something unacceptable happens. No one worries about good things happening to them – we only seek explanations for negative results and experiences. "Why bad things happen to good people" is a question that constantly bothers us. For example, your only child may have a terminal illness, or you fought in the recent election and lost. Or some charge was registered against you, so the police arrested you and drove you to the nearest police station. Or perhaps you and your wife had a quarrel and decided to divorce. Any of these things can happen. We all may wonder at such times, "Why do bad things happen to me?" You cannot change the event, because it has already happened. Now, how do you understand the situation and integrate such experiences?

When something happens, that defies rational explanation, which you cannot change, our tendency is to explain the event in terms of the unknown or the past. You think, "This is the result of something which I have done in the past. I am paying my dues. Maybe, in my past life, I stole someone's car, and due to that my car has been stolen, not once but twice! I am paying my *karmic* debt with compound interest."

Or you might have entertained the thought of stealing someone's car. That thought is introduced and is running about to find a host. Thought cannot remain long in emptiness, without fulfillment. It is running around in search of a host or a victim, but so far nothing has worked because others all have good *karma*. Finally, after a long, long search, unable to find a victim, the thought comes back and *your car* is stolen – because you are the one who initiated the thought.

Therefore, when you think of stealing someone's car, think again! Even if you think of stealing his car, later on your car will be stolen. *Karma* will return to you like a wrongly addressed letter. It goes around and finally comes back to the sender. Thoughts will come back to you and take their toll.

We have to be very careful about what thoughts we entertain, because we are introducing something into the cosmos, creating disturbances in the cosmic mind. Finally, thought has to manifest somewhere. You become the recipient of the product of that thought because, only that way, is the loop completed. "He who sows wind reaps a whirlwind," the proverb warns.

The intender receives the final fruit. When something bad happens to me that I cannot explain or avoid – for example, let us say a child who is born retarded – what can one do? At such times (like Sita) you have to accept it as your *karma*, your fate or *vidhi*. Maybe something that you or the child did in the past resulted in the present situation.

Some of the things which you cannot change, that are unfolding in your life today, can be explained in terms of the past. When you establish a reason, your mind settles down. Otherwise your mind will keep on asking, "Why did it happen? Why did it happen to me?" When you say, "I am responsible for this. I am paying back my old debts." Then your mind finds a rational explanation and settles down.

This is the first application of the *Law of Karma*: to understand that what happens today, which you cannot change, is the result of your past *karma*, your past thought and actions. This thought releases a lot of energy: "I am clearing my debts." You have a healthy feeling, "I am paying back my debts." When you become clear of unwanted debt, your credit-worthiness increases, and your stock rises in the "*karmic* market"! Otherwise your stock plummets.

Creating your Destiny

Another application of *karma* theory is that, "If the actions I undertake produce certain results, then, keeping the outcome in mind, I can modify my present actions." If you want to lead a happy life, you must do such deeds today that will create happy experiences in the future. If you want everyone to be kind to you and smiling, then plant seeds of positive behavior. When you send happy thoughts, they will have come back to you as happy experiences. Determine your present actions based upon whatever your ideals are for the future.

You have the power to modify your present thoughts and actions knowing that they will determine your future. That is taking charge of your life. No one can change that which has already happened, but you can reflect upon your past, interpret it, learn from it, and then choose your actions at any moment. Because the future depends upon what you do today, you create your own destiny. Depending upon how you interpret your present, and how you derive knowledge from it, you modify your future.

I heard a beautiful saying by a Christian saint, "O Lord, give me the power to accept what I cannot change, the power to change whatever I can, and the wisdom to know the difference." We have the power to choose our responses to past events and their results.

For example, some time ago you may have done something wrong and were sent to prison. However, even though you may think of prison as a punishment, it actually provides a new opportunity for you. It depends upon how you choose to respond to that situation.

Mahatma Gandhi and Nehru were put into jail. Neither of them sat down and cried. Rather, they saw their circumstances as an opportunity, a chance to escape from the crowds, read and produce their own books. Nehru wrote all his books while in jail – *Discovery of India*, *Glimpses of World History*, *Letter from Father to Daughter*, and other books for which he is remembered today. In fact, he is remembered more for the books he wrote while in jail than for his prime ministerial tenure. When you reap a particular result, choose an appropriate response to that result. See an opportunity in your circumstances whatever they are.

Although one use of *karma* is to explain your past, don't stop with the thought that, "I am merely paying back my past debt." Make use of the present situation by choosing appropriate responses. You have the inner power. Don't get cowed down by the past. Choose a response that will help you grow. When your car is stolen, it's an opportunity for you to get some exercise or to buy a new and better car. If you break your leg, it may be due to past misdeeds. You can submit to it and forget about it, or you can choose to think in a new way. Your broken leg may present an opportunity for you to discover a new devise for other disabled people to walk. While you are recuperating, you design an artificial limb and later learn to dance.

Once there was such a lady who danced with artificial limbs, and her dance was most exquisite. People crowded around her, seeing her dance using an artificial limb, amazed at the power of the human spirit. A person dancing with two legs is nothing novel. But someone who dances on artificial limbs is a rarity and a marvel. *Karma* is an opportunity, nature's way of bringing new energy into the world. *Karma* is a means for manifesting the spirit anew, for constant and fundamental renewal.

Opportunity in Calamity

The spirit can never be cowed down. Setbacks become opportunities for us to explore into the infinitude of the Spirit. For such adventurous people, every calamity represents an opportunity. For someone else, every opportunity is a calamity. If someone pushes you into a swimming pool and you know how to swim, the occasion represents an opportunity. You are happy because your were hesitating on the brink, and his push helped you to make up your mind! However, if you haven't learned to swim, what happens? Such an opportunity does not inspire you, because water cannot become a means for your self-exploration. Water invites a swimmer to leap in, explore his inner potential, and enjoy what he knows. A person who has no knowledge of swimming may shout and kick and finally drown. But if you are pushed unawares into the water, why not take it calmly and use the occasion as an opportunity to learn how to swim?

For a person who believes in the *Law of Karma*, every calamity is an opportunity. When Lord Rama was sent to the forest, he took it as an opportunity. Everybody else was angry, but Rama said, "This is my mission." Each of us has a mission to be discovered in this turbulent world. There are two ways: One is to take charge of your life and try to perform right action. Determine your actions based upon the outcome you want to create. If you want a happy outcome, create a happy situation. Since we have that ability to project the consequences, we have the power to make right choices.

Taking Charge of your Destiny

Kalidasa, the shepherd, was sitting on a limb of a tree and cutting the wrong end of the branch. A passerby saw what he was doing and shouted, "Fool, what are you doing, sitting on the branch and cutting on the side nearer to the tree trunk? You'll fall." Kalidasa asked, "How do you know?" This passerby did not say more and walked on. After some time the passerby saw this shepherd who had been sitting in the tree running towards him. When the shepherd reached him, he fell at his feet and cried, "You are *Bhagavan*! How did you predict that I was going to fall down?"

Sometimes, like Kalidasa, we are unable to connect causes and consequences, but a person who can connect them can clearly see the future. When your children don't study and indulge in idle pursuits, does the child clearly see the consequences? No, but you do! When you scold, the child will whine and complain, "My mother hates me!" You clearly see the danger, because you have the inner vision whereby you connect these two events, cause and effect in space-time, but the child cannot predict consequences. Similarly, an individual who can foresee the consequence of an act and also interpret his past can mold his actions according to the desired result. He learns lessons, and in his hand the past and the future become fluid. He becomes a master and a creator of his destiny. The *Law of Karma* does not make you impotent as a person. It puts the reins of your life into your hands. When you take charge, every natural force will support you.

Analyzing Fatalism

Some people think that whatever happens today and will happen in the future has already been predetermined. This is a fatalistic interpretation of *karma*. That means the present offers no options; you cannot do anything now about the future. Whether I make an effort or not, my fate is already written. This presents a very suicidal and erroneous interpretation of *karma*, betraying an attitude bereft of practical experience. *Karma* does not work like that. The *Law of Karma* says, "You are the deciding factor. You make choices moment to moment and *determine* your destiny."

Theoretically, *karma* explains your suffering in terms of your past behavior and choices that you made. But very few individuals are capable of probing relentlessly into the infinite past! However, those who are capable, grasp an explanation for their present condition. Essentially and ultimately, *karma* means that you are your best friend, and you are your own worst foe: "*atm'aiva hy atmano bandhur atm'aiva ripur atmanah*" (*Bhagavad Gita*. 6:5).

Limited Action Produces Limited Results

Action is bound by a beginning and an end. Whatever you start has to be limited, because no action can be infinite. Since action is limited, it will produce only limited results. You cannot be endlessly suffering due to one action, unlike the Biblical concept of eternal suffering in a Hell, or Adam and Eve's sin in the Garden of Eden condemning mankind eternally.

For the rest of all humanity's existence, we suffer the consequences of our first parent's singular action! Does it make any sense? For one limited action you cannot have an endless result. That way everyone may also be eternally happy. Put 100 dollars in the bank. Can you keep taking the $100 out eternally? No. Since action is finite, the result has to be finite. One does not suffer (or enjoy) endlessly due to past *karmas*.

Empowered by Karma

Finally, because of *karma* and its complexities, by experiencing good and bad, over a period of time you become a mature person. Ordinarily, you explain every experience or result in terms of good and bad, pleasure and pain. Suppose you go to the movies and you don't find a parking space. You complain, "My bad *karma.*" You explain everything with that word. When your children are not listening to your advice, you despair, "My bad *karma.*" When you continuously interpret everything in terms of "good" or "bad," it simply means *you* have performed good and bad deeds in the past – "As the effect, so the cause" – "As you sow, so shall you reap!" That is a law. If you are enjoying life, that is because of your past good deeds.

If you want to create a happy environment in the future, do something today to make it happen. You have that power. You can change your attitude and your vision and take charge of your life. That is what the *karma* theory *actually* says. *Karma* theory empowers. Ultimately, the same *karma* that made you feel inhibited will help you transcend the wheel of life. Through the cycle of pain and pleasure a situation will come when you understand the limitations of the whole mechanism, and you will step off the wheel of *karma* and *karma phala*. That is called *moksa*.

You must have seen children riding in a Ferris wheel? Children are put in little cage-like boxes attached to two wheels. Once they are inside, they cannot get out but sit in a chair, holding tightly to a bar with their legs dangling in mid-air. When the motor starts, the wheels turn and the little boxes go round and round, up and down. As the children go up, they laugh, "Ha, ha." When they come down, they giggle, "Hee, hee." Sankara says that this is a description of the human situation. Life is a series of these expressions – "Ha, ha" while going up, and "Hee, hee," while coming down. Helplessly, we are taken up and down – and, for that ride you also have to pay! It's not free. Then a time comes when you just don't submit to the ups and downs. You are released – because you know that *karma* is only a Ferris wheel ride going round and round, up and down, "Ha, ha," and "Hee, hee." Now you are an enlightened, wise "*swami*," "one who knows Truth," "who knows the infinite Self." Meanwhile, children still want to get into the Ferris wheel and ride on and on. However, once you discover your true nature, your "rootedness" in Pure Consciousness, this *Law of Karma* – this mechanism of cause and consequence – can be used creatively to enjoy the play of life.

Five

The Spiritual Law of Yajna

The Macrocosmic and Microcosmic Yajna

When you look around at all the glory of nature and wonderful achievements of humankind, everywhere you find that everything and everyone exists for something or someone else. Like a mother caring for her children and sacrificing her own needs for their sake. Like the trees that expire oxygen, and we human beings who expire carbon dioxide – everything is interdependent, sacrificing for each other. This is the *Law of Yajna*, the *Law of Sacrifice*, operating. This wonderful *Law* pervades every aspect of the cosmos and every operation in the world.

The mighty and glorious Sun, Earth's nearby star and independent source of light and heat, constantly converts hydrogen gases into helium in a combustion process that warms our globe. We take the sun for granted; only physicists truly understand the process. We are only vaguely aware that the sun is slowly and continuously burning itself out. Nor is the sun worrying on its own behalf, "If I burn at this rate, how long will I last?" The sun is there to burn itself out, and in that process it is giving light and life to our entire solar system. That is its destiny – to sacrifice. And sacrifice gives fulfillment. So, *yajna* exists at the very center of our solar system.

Another *yajna* is going on at the individual, microcosmic level. This is the sacrifice that the sense organs continuously perform as the ground of our physical existence. All the five sense organs are continuously pouring sensations into that Consciousness which you are. Suppose all sensations were taken away – your sight, or hearing, touch, smell, or taste – of what use would life be? It is impossible to live without sensations. They are necessary food for individual consciousness.

Sacrifice also goes on in a family. The mother is the center, the one who sacrifices her precious energy for the solidarity, survival, health and growth of the family. Children will not sacrifice, not even one wee bit. When you suggest they sacrifice, do without a particular thing, they retort, "It's your problem, not mine. Why did you bring me into this world?" The older generation could not even think of such responses! The man of the house may sacrifice his life for a career, but at home he sits on an easy chair, reading a newspaper and expects cups and cups of coffee. The whole family holds together due to the mother's sacrifice. When the mother is away or dies the family withers, because there is no central hub, no center of attraction for the entire family. In family life, the individual cognitive life, and the cosmic solar system – in all these three systems we find the *Law of Sacrifice* being continuously applied.

Nature is full of sacrifice. Take the example of the tree. The tree is constantly cleaning the air: you breathe out carbon molecules, and the tree "breathes" in the carbon molecules and breathes out the oxygen molecules. But for the tree, we would be unable to breathe; the trees are our lungs. We and the trees need one another to coexist. Not only for breathing, but without plants and trees, what would we eat? We cannot survive on stones. Through the process of photosynthesis, the leaves convert sunlight into tissues and produce edible food and medicine for creatures in the form of roots, leaves and fruit. You may deny the survival value of plants, insisting, "I am *not* a vegetarian; I don't require plants for food." Sir, if you are a non-vegetarian, you are eating cows, goats, snakes, and snails – anything that crawls or runs away from you. Then how do *those* creatures live? The cow or goat or pig that you eat, live on vegetables and grasses. You are merely eating double cooked vegetables!

We survive at the sacrifice of the plant kingdom. The plants give us food, medicine, shelter and protection. Suppose you are driving down the highway. Tired and hot and in need of some rest, you stop to sit under the cool comfort of a shade tree and enjoy the breeze.

Finally, the tree makes a total sacrifice, allowing itself to be cut into pieces so that you can build a house and fill your home with furniture. If you are a Christian, even your coffin is made from the tree. And, if you are a Hindu, trees supply the fuel for your funeral pyre.

A river's destiny – its ambition and dream – is to flow down towards the ocean, empty itself and disappear, sacrificing its identity. The ocean again sacrifices itself, becoming vapor and clouds. The clouds sacrifice for the earth, giving up their vapor to become the rain. Water and earth sacrifice together, nourishing the plants, trees and creatures. The whole of nature flows in the performance of *yajna*.

Sacrifice and Affluence

I call this flow of life "affluence," and the flow of life is only possible because of sacrifice. Someone sacrifices for someone else and finds fulfillment in that. Because of Mahatma Gandhi and the freedom fighters, who sacrificed their lives, India is enjoying freedom. Without their sacrifice freedom was impossible. When terrorists flew civilian airplanes into New York's "twin towers," 300 fire fighters sacrificed their lives. They knew these buildings were on fire and that the building might collapse at any time. But civilians were either trapped or trying to make their way out of the buildings, and it is the firefighter's duty to save those innocent civilians' lives. That means risking their own lives. They have been trained for that "supreme sacrifice." These 300 firefighters, knowing that their lives were in danger, walked into the smoking and burning World Trade Center, with oxygen cylinders and heavy equipment flung over their shoulders, for the sole purpose of saving lives. Flames and smoke surrounded them, and when the buildings collapsed, they were buried alive. Those kinds of sacrifices make a nation great. When we even think about those sacrifices, our hair stands on end. They were faithful to the dispensation of their duty. They had been trained for this moment of supreme sacrifice. Bravely facing their destiny, the firefighters and rescue workers found fulfillment. You and I would run away.

Understand that this *Law of Sacrifice* operates in every aspect of life. We human beings are conscious choice-makers. It is our capacity and freedom to either flout or abide by the *Law of Sacrifice.* In skirting the law there is temporary pleasure – that is why, in fact, we do try to escape from duty. As a fireman, there is no pleasure in jumping into the fire, and out of fear many of us would run away. Total fulfillment is lost in the fleeting pleasure of escape. Of course, such workers could retreat to their families and sleep in the safety of their homes. But once having skirted their duty, what kind of sleep will they get? But if you follow the law, and lose your precious life as a result, in its place you gain immortality! If the firemen had run away from that situation they may have saved their tiny, perishable lives, but they would have lost their opportunity for immortality. Thereafter, having shirked one's duty, life will feel empty and miserable. We can flout the law and suffer or follow the law and prosper; the choice is ours.

Giving and Receiving

Nature is very rich because it is based on this *Law of Sacrifice*. Everywhere this law is operating. What does that law say? That law says: "*To receive is to give*!" It appears to be a simple statement. Whatever you want to receive, first give. You receive only what you give. What you lose becomes your gain. As the scriptures say, "He who would lose his life, gains it." One who sacrifices gains immortality. Unless you lose your petty life, how will you gain immortality? How will you gain the feeling of fulfillment and timelessness? One has to sacrifice oneself. One has to lose the small, limited, physical life in order to discover the immortal life. That is why it is said, "To give is to gain; to lose is to discover." When you lose yourself – your little self, whatever you are today – you will discover your full potential.

Unless the seed falls on the ground and becomes buried in the earth and softened, unless the seed 'becomes excited' by the elements and water and breaks out of its hard shell, the seed cannot fulfill its potential. The seed's discovery of its potential and its fulfillment depends upon its yielding, its surrendering and offering up itself. Unless it offers itself to higher possibilities, for a higher ideal and higher satisfaction, it will never discover its potential and yield its blessings.

Most of us don't want to surrender anything we possess. The *Law of Yajna* says that whatever you try to possess, will perish in your hands; conversely, whatever you give or share will flourish and come back to you. These are extensions of that law. If you want to flourish don't possess.

The *Isavasya Upanishad* says, "*Isavasyam idam sarvam yatkinca jagatyam jagat; tena tyaktena bhunjitah*" (1) "The world belongs to God, therefore, renounce and rejoice. Possess and perish." Possession (in greed, or by hoarding) becomes a huge burden. When you renounce, you can rejoice. Experience will give us proof of that.

Once upon a time, as a youth in India, when you owned nothing, you were very free and happy. You walked into anyone's home as if it were your own, jumped into anyone's car without a care. If you had no kitchen, you could go into anyone's kitchen and eat for free. The child-like freedom of a *sannyasi* is immortalized in this brief statement from Sankaracharya's *Kaupina Panchakam*: "*Kaupina vanta khalu bhagyavanta*" – "He who owns nothing is happy." With much difficulty you built a house, bought a car and set up your kitchen. Thereafter, all your problems began. Now you own a home in America, the land of the free, but you are strapped with loan payments! You have to take up three jobs and work 18 hours a day to repay the debt. You estimate that you will need to work for 20 extra years, beyond normal retirement age, and are seldom at home to enjoy what you have. Who is enjoying your home? The housekeeper or the servant is!

Water that flows constantly remains fresh. But if water becomes stagnant, it loses its freshness and becomes stale.

Bacteria and disease breed in stagnant water. One has to keep giving; the more you flow, the more you grow. The *Law of Sacrifice* mandates that by giving you flourish, by possessing you will perish. Give first and then receive. Those alone who sacrifice flourish; they alone progress and find their final fulfillment.

The Meaning of Yajna

The word for sacrifice in Sanskrit is *yajna*. Its root syllable is "*yaj*" meaning "to offer, sacrifice." *Yajna* is a wonderful concept. The whole philosophy of sacrifice is encapsulated in that single word *yajna*. In the *Bhagavad Gita* Krishna says, "*Yajn'arthat karmano'nyatra / loko'yam karma bandhanah / tad-artham karma Kaunteya / mukta-sangah samacara*" (3:9). "Work as an offering is liberating; any other attitude makes work constricting." Any activity undertaken with selfish intentions will bind you. The more you engage in selfish activities, the more you will be bound. Here, by adopting the *yajna* attitude, the more you work the more you are liberated from your limitations, tensions and excitements.

There are two lifestyles. One is a lifestyle based upon self-sacrifice. The other is a life based upon self-aggrandizement. Most of us follow that materialistic law – give little and take the maximum. Whereas, spiritual law says, "Give more, and what you give, that alone, will come back to you." For example, let us examine the life of a farmer: he knows the seed that he is throwing on fertile soil will come back to him a thousandfold bringing him a rich harvest and dividend. On the contrary, if the farmer were to think, "How can I trust nature? What guarantee is there that, if I sow these seeds, they will yield any return? I'll keep all these seeds in a plastic bag, put it in an iron trunk and keep the key in my pocket." How ridiculous! If the farmer does that, after some time, he will find out that the seeds become stale and unworthy of even consumption. The best law in life, the farmer knows, is first to sacrifice; first give and then receive. Now our problem is, "What should I give?"

Giving Your Best

Swami Vivekananda once told this story: A young man came to him requesting *sannyas.* He said, "Swamiji, I heard that *sannyas* is the highest ideal, and I trust you. I want to become a *sannyasi.*" Vivekananda said, "That is great. I have been searching for such young people, who are ready to sacrifice themselves for a higher spiritual attainment. But, may I ask you one question? Do you have something to sacrifice? Do you know typing, or bookkeeping, or cooking? What are your skills and training?" "I know nothing, Swamiji; that's why I want to become a *sannyasi.* Otherwise, why would I come here asking you to give me *sannyas*?" Swamiji chided the silly young man, "If you have nothing to renounce, how can you be a *sannyasi*?"

To renounce, you must have something to renounce. Each one of you is unique and possesses talents. Your contribution is your renunciation. Few people want to contribute their hard-earned money to the wealth of the nation, and yet everyone wants their share from the government. Such a nation will only distribute poverty rather than wealth. The first principle of sacrifice is that you must have something to sacrifice. If you have nothing to sacrifice, then sacrifice has no meaning at all. Those who want to sacrifice must train and prepare themselves so that they are worthy of sacrifice.

In olden times, the best sheep in your flock or the best product of your field was sacrificed to God – not the most useless animal or a spoiled fruit! Nowadays it is the opposite; when devotees buy fruit and see that one which they have taken is spoiled, they think, "What will I do with this one? No one will relish it. Why not place this fruit on the temple altar and offer it to God? They will give it to some poor beggar." Don't behave like this – that which you offer should be the best!

Once upon a time, the best men were literally sacrificed on the altar. After a long wait and supplication to the Lord, the Biblical Abraham, had a son, whom he named Isaac. When he was born, God commanded Abraham, "I want a sacrifice. I want a proof of your devotion. Sacrifice your son, Isaac, for my sake." Of course it was a very difficult command for

Abraham to carry out. Finally he decided, "That is true. My son is a gift from God, and he is the best thing I have to offer. I will follow God's command and sacrifice Isaac." Abraham took his son to the mountaintop and, there, laid him on the slab of stone, looked up into the heavens, and closing his eyes, raised his sword poised to sacrifice his precious son. At that moment, he suddenly heard a bleating sound. He looked around to see where the cry had come from, and saw a goat standing nearby. Then an invisible voice declared, "Release Isaac and instead sacrifice this goat."

Abraham's intention, his readiness and willingness to sacrifice was very important. That was the secret of his strength of character and personality. The whole of Abrahamic religious tradition – with three billion adherents, including Jews, Christians and Moslems – is based upon that un-conditional sacrifice which Abraham was ready to offer at God's altar.

Similarly, we find in the Western tradition, the sacrifice of Jesus Christ – God sacrificing his only begotten son. Christ, God's "only begotten Son," was sacrificed for humankind's sake and crucified on the cross. It was not a just punishment; he did not commit any sin. He was not suffering any punishment for misdeeds; rather, because of his love and his sense of duty, he sacrificed himself – and the whole of Christendom is built upon Christ's sacrifice.

Indian Examples of Sacrifice

In India also you find such instances of sacrifice. For the sake of his father, Rama sacrificed his throne and went to live in the forest. He could have insisted, "No, no. My father is senile and wrongly influenced by his wife; he does not know what he is saying. I refuse to go!" Instead, Rama said, "I am ready to willingly sacrifice, because my father has given his word, and I must help my father fulfill his promise and move to the forest." Due to his sacrifice Rama became immortal.

Although Sri Krishna fought many battles and won many victories, he never coveted the throne. He was always a sacrificing god. Krishna fought because his joy was in the very sacrifice itself, and left the spoils and afterglow of victory for lesser mortals to enjoy!

There is also the example of Dadhiji in the *Puranas*. Indra wanted a new weapon to fight against the *asuras* (demons) and went to Vishnu for help. Vishnu instructed him, "Go to Dadhiji, who has been doing extensive *tapas*, and ask him for one of his ribs." Indra wondered, "How is this possible?" Vishnu added, "You will come to know Dadhiji and understand his value system. Go prostrate before him, and ask him for his rib bone, and he will give it to you." With much hesitation, Indra went and fell at the feet of Dadhiji and asked, "I need one of your ribs in order to forge a new weapon to defend righteousness." Dadhiji replied happily, "Take it," and in an instance of great sacrifice Dadhiji self-immolated, leaving his rib for Indra.

Similarly, one day, King Sibi of Kashi, was sitting on his throne when a little dove came and sat on his lap, shaking and frightened. Then Sibi saw a vulture lurking nearby. The vulture addressed Sibi, "Maharaj, I am hungry and my breakfast is that little dove sitting in your lap. Please release my breakfast." But Sibi replied, "How can I give up this frightened little bird? You will eat him up. I cannot release him. As my citizen it is my job is to protect him." The vulture cleverly replied, "Maharaj, this dove may be a citizen of your country, but so am I! I also require sustenance." Now the Maharaj was in a real catch-22 situation, not knowing what to do. But the means by which he resolved that problem is worthy of our reflection. You and I would kill both birds and feast. But the Maharaj took flesh from his own thigh, offered it to the vulture and said, "Now, may both of you live." In doing so, he protected *both* the vulture and the dove. He didn't sacrifice one bird for the sake of the other; he sacrificed himself. This is what creates affluence in both our individual and collective life. By that simple act of direct resolve and sacrifice, Sibi satisfied both. He ensured peace and, in the process, attained total satisfaction for himself. Due to his sacrifice, he is immortalized.

You find such a multitude of stories in all cultures across the world, but today the "winner takes it all" philosophy thrives – a philosophy of greed and selfishness. As a result of this attitude, violence, dissatisfaction, and disharmony prevail in this world.

But if we all were to apply this *Law of Sacrifice*, not only would those who sacrifice obtain supreme fulfillment, but such acts of sacrifice would create a culture of affluence.

Simple Affluence

Sacrifice uplifts the general energy level of the world. In the long run, a "winner takes all" philosophy doesn't work. In fact, the *winner* is to be sacrificed! This ideal is expressed in our traditional Indian way of life. In India, as you rise up in the human hierarchy, you become a *sannyasi*. The highest cultural ideal is sacrifice or *sannyasa*. The *sannyasi* reduces his or her needs and comforts, lives simply and organizes his or her thought processes in accordance with these laws.

A manual worker requires a generous amount of food. But as one rises up reaching the higher echelons of power – like a Mahatma Gandhi – one's needs are very little. Lal Bahadur Shastri lived on a single glass of orange juice for breakfast and he was one of the best Prime Ministers that India ever saw. He didn't think, "Since I'm the Prime Minister; I must have a 6-egg omelet for breakfast." No doubt Bill Gates' needs are meager, though he is sitting on top of the heap – because he obtains tremendous satisfaction from what he is doing. One who sacrifices becomes immortal, and such a person gains final fulfillment.

The philosophy of sacrifice says, "Sacrifice for the sake of survival." The *Gita* proclaims, "*Yajna-dana-tapah karma / na tyajyam c'apare*" (18:3). "Don't give up these three values: *yajna* or sacrifice, *dana* or sharing, and *tapa* or discipline." These three values are vital to human survival. A society that lives these principles becomes an affluent and glorious society.

Through a life of sacrifice, because you take only what is necessary, you create material affluence and social harmony. In first giving and then taking one creates a flowing field of energy. If you simply take and do not give, that flow is cut off and affluence subsides. Through a life of sacrifice, not only will you attain inner peace, but you will also unfold your total, human potential.

By living this life of sacrifice, all values that we seek are ensured. The creation of wealth, social equity, peace and justice, inner peace and the experience of total unfoldment of our inner potential – all these, and more, are achieved in living this simple *Law of Sacrifice*. First give and then take. Lose yourself, to save yourself. If you hoard or accumulate greedily, you perish.

Sacrifice and Excellence

The next question is: what do I sacrifice? Sacrifice the best! But, do I have *the best* to give? To become the best, you must discipline yourself. Without discipline there is nothing to sacrifice. For sacrifice you must pursue excellence. For example, take the martial arts. You discipline yourself in such a way that you are constantly pursuing excellence, and your own life is centered in that discipline. Finally, the martial artist, having continuously developed himself, sacrifices in the arena of competition. He pursues a goal, trying to find the limit of his excellence and power. He does not run away from a challenge, but engages himself in ever more complex and risky adventures. Life without pursuing excellence is not otherwise worthwhile for him. If we simply live without pursuing excellence, life loses its meaning. Sacrifice means relentlessly pursuing excellence.

A worthy "sacrificer" excels in some field. Otherwise one is just *amedhya*, an incompetent person "unfit for sacrifice," like the rotten apple that cannot be offered for any higher purpose. In ancient religious traditions, an imperfect animal (for example, an animal whose leg is broken) was barred from being used as a sacrifice. You must be the best if you want to have the ecstasy of offering yourself at a higher altar! Like camphor, you want to burn down completely at the feet of the Lord, without a trace of residue. For that kind of excellence, like Arjuna, you must prepare yourself continuously.

During the *Mahabharata*, why did Krishna take Arjuna as his friend and his spiritual partner? Because Arjuna had the quality of relentlessly pursuing excellence! Krishna called Arjuna "*Parantapa*, "Scorcher of Enemies," "*Dhananjaya*," "Winner of Wealth," and "*Gudakesha*," "The Ever-Wakeful One." Once fascinated by an idea, or having learned a lesson from his *guru*,

Arjuna applied himself again and again until he perfected his skill. To be worthy of sacrifice, you must be a paragon of virtue and excellence.

Today we say, "O young men and women! Arise and sacrifice for your country!" But do they have something to sacrifice? They neither know medicine, nor engineering, nor language. The only thing they know is how to eat! Such people are a burden. To live the life of sacrifice, you must excel in some field. Then alone does your sacrifice become relevant.

The first principle of sacrifice is: train yourself and excel! This pursuit must become a passion for you. Take it as your *dharma*. Without that you will become only a nuisance to others. Even God will not want your sacrifice.

Once there was a devotee of the Lord who chanted, "Rama, Rama," all the time and did nothing else during his life. When he died, the *yamaduta* (assistants of *Lord Yama*) thought, "This man was constantly chanting 'Rama, Rama.' It may be that Rama will accept him. We will put him in Rama's company, in Vishnuloka." Then the *yamaduta* sent a message to Vishnu. "This person seems to be your ardent devotee. Would you like to accommodate him in your heavenly *loka*?" Vishnu pleaded, "Please don't send him here! I won't get a minute's sleep! Constantly chanting 'Rama Rama Rama,' he's nothing but a disturbance! He only chants and doesn't do a single minute's work, and I won't be able to do my work either! Send him elsewhere."

The idea is that if you are to sacrifice yourself, you must be a precious, unique person and excel in some field. Otherwise your offering has little meaning. Becoming the best requires disciplined effort and continuous and passionate training. You must also be able to work in association with others in order to explore your full potential. No one can fully develop in isolation. Development of your excellence is possible only when you rub shoulders with other excellent people.

Excellence in Association

The martial artist provides an image of internal standards. You can extrapolate from this example to all other fields. The martial arts require great body control. In the process of learning martial arts, one also gains mental control. But how about control over your emotions? Those controls are also necessary. Our problem is that when we are alone we are very excellent. But when we associate with others, then jealousy, anger, arrogance and all other negative emotions arise, and we become unable to function in such a situation. There is a famous saying: "One Indian is equal to ten Japanese; but ten Indians are equal to one Japanese!" Why so? Because, when ten Indian comes together, negative energy, "negergy," is created – no synergy at all!

To explore your own potential, you must be able to interact and work with other people of excellence. To become an absolutely excellent person, you must live and thrive in excellent company. This requires a lot of mental and emotional discipline. Without that control, your excellence cannot be achieved. When that discipline is in place, you are able to manage not only your psycho-physical personality, but also your relationships with others. Then, together, we can attain higher reaches of excellence.

The way we perfect ourselves is though interaction with other excellent people. In a martial arts academy, everyone is challenging each other – practicing, trying to grow and explore their abilities, having high standards and wanting to exceed the other person. Each nourishing the other, they are able to explore their higher potential. But if you went to the academy and you were the only student, what opportunity for excellence is possible? You must be willing to interact with other excellent people. Offer this work and receive the offering back. The *Gita* says, "*Saha yajnah prajah srstva / puro'vaca Prajapatih / anena prasavisyadhvam / esa vo'stv ishta-kamadhuk*" (*Gita*. 3:10) – "May you prosper by applying this law in your life, the *Law of Sacrifice*." The heart of *yajna* is to offer your work at a higher altar.

Prasadam

Krishna says "What you eat, without offering to God, is poison." If you straightaway eat, you are missing that opportunity to convert what you are eating into nectar. "*Istan bhogan hi vo deva / dasyante yajna-bhavitah / tair dattan apraday'aibhyo yo bhunkte stena eva sah, // Yajna-sist'asinah santo / mucyante sarva-kilbisaih / bhunjate te tv agham papa / ye pacanty atma karanat*" (*Gita*. 3:12-13). Krishna says, "Pleased by your offering, the gods bless you with choicest gifts, by sharing those gifts you make them twice blessed. He who eats alone eats poison." You can prosper, *prasavisyadhvam*; the greatest affluence can be created – psychological and social peace along with material affluence – by following this law.

A mutually nourishing and caring community is "*ishta kamadhuk*" – a wish-fulfilling cow. God has created us with this understanding and ability, but rarely do we cultivate or follow the law. For example, the American economy is a wish-fulfilling cow. Why? What is their secret? They apply the law of cooperative effort, and, offering that at the higher altar of democracy, they create affluence. That is the market economy – you bring your produce to the market and procure your needs from the market. Their altar may be material, but that doesn't matter. Application of this law – give and take – creates wealth. But if you make only whatever you require in your house, then there is no wealth creation or affluence.

Whatever is your offering, these principles are to be followed. Your offering comes back to you and to the people around you. We offer fruits or sweetmeats to the temple deity, and close our eyes. When we close our eyes, if Ganesha ate up everything, next time we won't offer much; instead we will divide it – "One for Ganesha, and the rest for me. Ordinarily, we offer the whole of it at the altar, Ganesha blesses it, and then we receive it back from him. What the Lord gives back to us is *prasadam*. You need a subtle sensibility to perceive that. Nothing apparent has taken place. The same quantity you gave and kept there – perhaps just a single *tulasi* leaf – is given back to you. Essentially, nothing has happened, but you have energized the offering. Out of poison, you have made nectar.

The life of sacrifice creates a climate of health, wealth, affluence and peace. The law says: "First give, and then take." Then alone can you be a free person. Otherwise you create misery in the world.

Yajna: *Our Cosmic Connectedness*

Most of us do not understand all the implications involved in *yajna*. There are cosmic gods (or cosmic energies, if you prefer) you can connect with and implore those powers and propitiate the deities by performing rituals. The best way to propitiate these powers, of course, is by an act of self-offering. You offer yourself, your excellence. *Yajna* is another method. In the *yajnasala* (where *puja* or rituals using material offerings are given) the concept is that we are propitiating certain deities. The priests chant, "*Indraya svaha; Varunaya svaha*," etc., as we make our offerings. As a result, the gods are pleased. That is why the *Bhagavad Gita* says, "*Devan bhavayat'anena te deva bhavayantu vah / parasparam bhavatyantah...*" (3:11). "If you please the gods, they in turn nourish and cherish you." They bring rain and grant victories, and provide you with plenty (cows). These are all metaphorical ways of presenting the application of this law.

In the application of the *Law of Yajna*, five stages are to be understood: 1) prepare yourself, intellectually, psychologically and physically; 2) engage with other excellent people, together creating an atmosphere of excellence; 3) offer this collective work at the altar of a higher ideal and receive the result; 4) share the results; and, 5) whatever balance remains keep as your profit. This is the spirit and law of prosperity.

If you witness a *yajna*, what do you see? The center of the *yajnasala* is the fire, the eternal symbol of sacrifice. Four priests sit around the fire, each presiding over a specific function of the *yajna*. The *adhvaryu* knows the technology of organizing a *yajna*. He specializes in preparing the material and altar; the *hota* makes the offering; the *udgatha* chants the hymns and *mantras*; and, the *Brahman* superintends. The *yajna* begins with the chanting of *mantras*.

When the fire is lit, seven tongues of fire are distinguishable. Each flame has a name – "*Kali karali ca manojava ca / sulohitha ya ca sudhumravarna // Sphulingini visvaruci . . . iti saptajjivah*" (*Mundaka Upanishad*. I.ii.4). "Kali, Karali, Manojava,

Soluhita, Sudhumravarna, Sphulingini and bright Visvaruci – these are the seven playful tongues of the fire." Each tongue represents a deity. Suppose you say, "*Indraya svaha,*" and then offer the ghee to a different flame. Then the offering goes somewhere other than where it should. *Indra* is waiting for it, but some other deity receives it instead!

Such a case would be similar to your college days, when you wrote a love letter to your girl friend but addressed it wrongly. By mistake it ends up in your father's hands – a real calamity. Your father never expected to read such a letter – even though he may have done that when he was a student! Like father like son! But that is a different problem. He has very conveniently forgotten *his own* youth! When he reads the letter, he threatens to take away your mobile phone and considers taking your car and the car keys, as well! There are stiff consequences when what is supposed to be offered to one person ends up in the hands of the wrong party!

Likewise, it is very important that the *hota* knows what item is to be offered to which flame. The *udgatha* chants the *mantra* – and he should know which *mantra* to chant! Suppose that while making offerings to a particular flame meant for a certain deity, the *udgatha* chants an unrelated *mantra*. The offering is meant for Ganesha but he chants the *mantra* for Vishnu. *Deva loka* will plunge into utter confusion. Petitions are going to wrong *devas*, demands are made for wrong *lokas*, and offerings are made to wrong gods! And because these deities are the ones who protect us, when there is confusion in *deva loka*, confusion will reign on Earth as well!

Through our sacrifices we provide for the gods. Who is paying the salary for the Prime Minister, the Members of Parliament and the President? You and I are! They are supposed to look after our welfare, so we must pay them to do their job. Similarly, through sacrifice we provide for the *devas*; thereafter, they protect us and provide for us. But if you commit all these errors – you fail to pay your taxes (i.e. no sacrifices) – what will the government do?

Once, in the state of Kerala, no salary was available for any legislator or government employees because no citizen paid their taxes. Unremunerated government officials become lax and ineffective in their governance. Such a situation creates a great deal of confusion, and the problem becomes a vicious circle. To create a *virtuous* cycle again is very difficult! Falling is very easy; rebuilding is difficult. Therefore, it is vital that the *hota* knows what to offer where, and that the *udgatha* knows what to chant.

Supervising all this, you have the *Brahman*, another priest. The *Brahman* doesn't speak much while in the *yajnasala*. He just observes. He is like the Indian President who will speak only when some crisis occurs. Or he is like an emergency light: when regular power fails, the emergency light powers up. Similarly, the *Brahman*, seated in the *yajnasala*, supervises the *yajna*. He generally doesn't say anything. But, only when something goes wrong, he utters, "*Om.*" If everything is going okay, he responds with encouragement, "*Om, Om.*" He is not to utter anything else in any other circumstances while the *yajna* is being performed. All the other priests are supposed to be actively engaged, doing their duties carefully and properly.

Success in Cooperation

When the priests work in coordination with one another, the *yajna* is successful. The right material, the right method of offering, the right *mantra* being chanted – for whose sake are all these offerings being done? The offerings are given to propitiate gods Indra, Varuna, Marutah – all the deities who superintend the cosmos. Unfortunately we don't have the subtlety to see or experience these deities. We say, "Show me that god." I cannot show you any one of these gods! They are invisible, but you can see the result of their having been propitiated and having carried out their functions and duties. A doctor will give you medicine and you may not actually *see* it work but you do experience the result.

A similar modern concept of *yajna* is all of us working together cooperatively, for example, as we worked under the leadership of Mahatma Gandhi. Gandhi represents *Brahman* in the *yajna*. All others, metaphorically, are various priests. Cherishing the higher ideal of independence, all of us worked under the leadership of Mahatma Gandhi. Independence is a *deva*. Although one cannot draw a picture of independence, we experience it as a blessing. Metaphorically you may use two flying birds to denote independence or a flower blooming, but we cannot have an actual picture of an abstract concept, only a metaphor.

Therefore, independence is a like a *deva*, and all of us offered our work at the altar of that *deva*. This was done consistently, and one day, the gods smiled upon us – that is, Britain granted our country freedom – not that they wanted to, but they just decided to "quit" in despair. The gods smiled upon our *yajna* and blessed us, and we became a free and independent nation. Once the gods give you freedom; don't stop cherishing and nourishing them, thereafter. Continue offering *yajna*, so that you can attain higher and higher achievements.

Our problem is that one fluke success goes into our heads. We are free and think that there is nothing more to be done. No. The cosmic powers are to be shown gratitude for our success and to be sustained with further *yajna*. Krishna said it very clearly in the *Bhagavad Gita*, "When success comes, appreciate and propitiate the gods again. Don't egoistically claim that any success is due to your personal action."

Mahatma Gandhi followed that principle, never claiming that success belonged to him. When everyone else was celebrating India's Independence, giving speeches and congratulations in Delhi, the architect of that independence – this frail old man of 78 – was in Naokhali, an obscure Bengali village, negotiating across a rickety bridge. Even his high blood pressure (due to the fight between Nehru and Patel) did not stop his work. He left the celebrating of independence to others. This is the meaning and significance of sacrifice.

One who sacrifices will not sit back to enjoy the fruit; that is for lesser mortals. He goes on making more sacrifices. The more he sacrifices, the more continuously he is fulfilled. The more he becomes fulfilled, the more he sacrifices. What a wonderful way to live! This is akin to *sannyasa*.

Three Levels of Sannyas

There are three stages in *sannyasa*. The first is when you give up your home and concerns of the home to become a *sannyasi*. Such an individual is restless with the ordinary life style; he wants to walk chasing the horizon, to see what lies beyond. He experiences a higher calling that he is unable to articulate. Responding to that call, he walks onward and becomes a *sannyasi*. Now, everyone appreciates and even worships him. A few devotees gather around him. Someone donates land. Thereafter, he becomes a big "successful" *swami*.

The problem is that the same *swami*, who once walked into the horizon in search of a higher calling, is now stuck! His present problem is one of collecting money to sustain all his empire and doing whatever tricks have to be done to manage his large acquisition of property and *ashrams*! His success has trapped him. He again has to renounce, leave everything to others and walk off again. This is his second renunciation. The third renunciation is more subtle and takes place when even the "feeling" that you have renounced is also renounced. When one achieves that state, then he or she has become a real *sannyasi*.

Once, a thief broke into a palace, and as he was making away with the golden ornaments the guards saw him and chased him off. The thief ran, and finally, when he didn't know where to hide, he saw a small hut. He peeked inside and no one was there, just some ochre robes lying in the room. He did not know how to escape, so he put on the ochre robes and sat there "in *samadhi*," as he had no other escape route. By that time the palace guards arrived and entered the hut. They saw a *sannyasi* calmly sitting in lotus posture with his eyes closed, and they prostrated before him. In his "*samadhi*," the thief heard the footsteps of the guards, and their prostrating, and their getting up to leave! Then, having put on the ochre robes, the thief suddenly had second thoughts: "I am the thief, and they are prostrating to me simply because of this cloth! I should also live according to the values this cloth represents and tell the truth." When the guards were turning away, the newfound *sannyasi* spoke, "Good sirs, you are in search of the thief, aren't you? I admit – I am the thief." The guards prostrated again and said, "*Swami*, why do you take this sin upon yourself! Look, it is someone else's mistake, and you are taking it upon yourself!" Then they performed more prostrations.

Such is the true *sannyasi*, who renounces the notion of renunciation. When that happens, the third level of *sannyasa* – renunciation – has been accomplished. The meaning is that you have to perfect renunciation.

Once we go through these various stages of renunciation, the gods bless us. Then a partnership ensues between the gods and us. However, one success is not enough; sacrifice must continue. That is how you reach the horizon, how you reach perfection, and how you reach the depths and the greatest fulfillment. Thus, the greatest fulfillment, the greatest affluence, comes as a result of continuously practicing sacrifice. Make your whole life a continuous offering at the altar of perfection and, as a result of that, you create both affluence and peace in this world.

Krishna says, "*Esa vo'stv ishta-kamadhuk*" (*Gita*. 3:10). By adopting the *yajna* attitude and way of life, applying this *Law of Yajna*, "May you create infinite wealth." At the end of the *Bhagavad Gita*, Krishna again says the same thing – "*Yatra yog'esvarah Krsno / yatra Partho dhanur-dharah / tatra srir vijayo bhutir / dhruva nitir matir mama*" (18:78). "As a result of sacrifice and pursuit of excellence offered at the altar of higher principles, success, prosperity, justice and fairness abound."

Even in the *Mahabharata* you find that Dharmaputra and his brothers engage in the game of dice. That is, again, a spirit of sacrifice. Duryodhana challenged the Pandavas to a game of dice. The Pandavas could have said, "No, we don't want to take that risk; we are happy with what we have. May you also be happy with whatever you have." This was not the Pandavas' attitude. We often ask, "Why did Dharmaputra play the game of dice, knowing very well that Duryodhana is a devious person?" Because Dharmaputra followed this *Law of Sacrifice*, applying the law that implies, "Nothing that one possesses is so precious that it cannot be risked or given away." You must continue to challenge yourself, offer whatever you have, and if it comes back, fine. If it doesn't, then you don't deserve it.

Risk and Sacrifice

As someone once said, "The greatest risk is not taking any risk." We need to take risks and play the dice game, laying everything at the altar of uncertainty. This is the risk that Dharmaputra took. He thought, "The kingdom and kingly pleasures are impermanent. What is important for me is an attitude of sacrifice, taking everything to the altar of a higher pursuit, risk and uncertainty. If I place my offering there and I am deserving it will come back to me. If I don't deserve it, it will fade." There is another way of expressing this same attitude of sacrifice found in the *Bhagavad Gita*, "*Dyutam chalayatam asmi*" (*Gita*. 10:36). "Among games, I am the game of dice."

We ought to do as Dharmaputra did – take the ultimate in risk. There is a lot of excitement in that kind of life. Dharmaputra staked the kingdom, his brothers, his wife –

everyone was placed on this stake – and he lost everything! Instead of leading a quite, middle class, secure life, live like Dharmaputra and find opportunity in the new situation! He thought, "Now, let me have some discipline, or at least shed some weight!" When he lost everything in a game of dice, he pursued his new course gracefully. I tell you, it is better to lead such a life rather than hold onto these petty little things that you own and worry about. Throw everything on the altar of dice. Make life a game of dice!

The reason why Krishna says, "I am the game of dice," is because that game makes you risk everything. It makes you become a real *sannyasi*, a great sacrificer – and you knowingly walk into that uncertainty. Unless you have that great inner power, you will fall short of taking risks. You may risk 10 dollars worth of quarters when you go to Las Vegas. That is not real risk-taking. In real risk-taking there is a great ecstasy. While Dharmaputra put everything at stake others protested. Bhima did not understand. Arjuna, who himself was a great risk-taker, was baffled.

If you want to pursue excellence you must be capable of taking risks. This is the message of *Mahabharata*. In the forest, Dharmaputra learned all the great lessons of life. Finally he came back, won the battle against Duryodhana and became the king. He ruled for some time, and then, one fine day decided, "I am leaving,." Bhima said, "Are you my brother? Have you gone mad? Here is the kingdom. You have all the kingly pleasures for which you fought and spilt blood! Now you want to leave! What is wrong with you? Why this restlessness?"

Your restlessness is the whispering of eternity. What you already possess is not your final destination. You have to explore the horizon further and farther. Dharmaputra put out his sacrificial fire, loosened his hair and removed all his royal robes. Without any shoes or any passbook or credit card in hand, he left, with only a single *dhoti* wrapped around his waist! There are some *sannyasis* who won't give up their passbook or checkbook. That is not *sannyasa*. You are the same old worm! Under those conditions, you will not develop the wings to fly into the vast sky! Throw away your passbook and checkbook. Let someone else care for it, and without shoes, without any security, walk into the ample bosom of Mother Nature. That is called the risk, and in that risk there is ecstasy and fulfillment. Putting your self on the firing line, you even challenge God.

The Meaning of Sacrifice

Such people alone understand the meaning of sacrifice. Sacrifice is not throwing a pittance into a beggar's bowl; it means putting your life on the firing line, throwing yourself into an adventurous new world. And, the more you practice this, the more your life juices will start flowing. Don't think, "I am old; how can I do that?" In fact, *sannyasa* is prescribed as one attains old age. At the age of 75, our scripture says, "Leave home." That is a very bitter pill. You think, "Had I left home at age of 20, I can understand!" The *Shastras* say, "Study hard for 25 years (*brahmacharya*). Work hard for your family and society another 25 (*grihastha*). Then develop an inner life for the next 25 years (*vanaprastha*), and finally, at 75 years of age silently leave everything behind – because now you have wisdom! That is *sannyas*. This way you recreate life over and over and experience continuous transcendence.

Such miracles happen. At the age of 75, a woman decided (although she had never even hummed a tune) that she wanted to learn music. At the age of 80, your grandfather may want to become a cook or learn to paint. This way, we are never finished with life. We keep on moving. Thus, Krishna says, "I am that risk involved in the play of dice." The joy you get out of that supreme sacrifice is Me!" In supreme sacrifice, there is great joy.

These are the several dimensions of sacrifice. Sacrifice does not mean simply to offer some grain, or a rotten apple, or your 10 percent tithe at the temple. Sacrifice is a total pursuit of excellence and continuing to excel, having an ongoing passion for excellence and continuously offering your self at the *highest* altar. As in olden days – the best, *your best*, is sacrificed.

But in many quarters of the world, the winner takes it all. If you are the best, you use your power to grab from others and suppress them. Actually the most powerful person must lay his power at the service of the society, at the service of God. That is the highest ecstasy that one can have, the ecstasy of supreme sacrifice.

Apply this law and see what difference it makes. This is what our *Vedas* declare: "The ideal of supreme sacrifice is making life itself into a series of sacrifices." When you burn like a lump of camphor in front of the Lord, there is great ecstasy. By "in front of the Lord" I mean that you relentlessly pursue excellence, offering everything that you create out of your pursuit! When that happens, there is true ecstasy. Nothing short of this can give you the joy that you are seeking!

Six

The Spiritual Law of Yoga

The Spirit of Detachment

Few of us have experienced that ecstasy of love, of union or *yoga*, found in loving everyone. That love has to be realized, and that alone is true love. This love develops out of detachment. When you are detached, then you can truly love.

Most parents spoil their children because of their passionate, attached love. Due to a kind of fear psychosis and extreme attachment, frequently, Indian parents don't allow their children any degree of freedom and personal choice. In the process, children replicate that fear in their own responses to the world, clinging to their parents lifelong. And that is exactly what such parents want! In their effort to control and manipulate the children, parents make their children into parasites. And, as a consequence, even when the child grows up, he or she remains forever emotionally crippled and unable to discover his or her true potential.

To become all that you can be and experience true love, the

Law of Yoga, or the *Law of Detachment*, is to be applied lifelong. Detachment is the true and final meaning of *yoga*.

Let's now explore *yoga's* meaning and dynamics. The simple meaning of *yoga* is "non-reaction," whatever the situation may be. Lord Krishna says in the *Bhagavad Gita*, "*Sukha-duhkhe same kritva / labh'alabhau jay'ajayau / tato yuddhaya yujyasva / n'aivam papam avapsyasi*" (2:38). "Keeping the mind even in pleasure and pain, and in profit and loss, persevere in detachment; thus you will not incur sin." That ability to restrain reaction is *yoga*.

Ordinarily we think of *yoga* as meaning standing on your head, twisting your body into various contortions and impossible postures – a demonstrative *yoga*. That form of *yoga* (*hatha yoga*) is not the be-all or the end-all of *yoga*. The true *yoga* is restraining your reactions in both success and failure.

In the *Bhagavad Gita*, this word *yoga* is explored in detail and various definitions are given. One definition of *yoga* is, "Non-reaction to the fruit of your work" – "*Karmany ev'adhikaras te / ma phalesu kadacana*" (*Gita*. 2:47). "You have control over your action but not over the results! Although you can choose a course of action, determining the outcome of that action is not within your power.

For example, you and your friend plan to attend a concert held in the evening at the university, so you take a bath, put on fresh clothes and dash out the door to hail a taxi. You jump into the first taxi that pulls over to the curb, and you are on your way. Suddenly, the taxi breaks down, and the driver takes half an hour for repairs. By that time the concert is half over, so you decide, "Let's forget it. My stars aren't good today."

Although you had made a decision to attend the concert and pursued a course of action, an obstacle arose and you could not carry out your plan. When such things happen, Krishna's advice is, "Don't react." Accept it. Another time comes when you succeed. Even then, Krishna's advice is, "Don't react."

Since you cannot guarantee the outcome of your actions, when the results come, don't get upset and "lose your cool," so to speak. When success comes we hit the ceiling in jubilation; and when failure descends we slide down into the dumps. We feel either overwhelmed or *under*-whelmed – like a yoyo, winding up and down, swinging to and fro. But the true *yogi* doesn't undergo such swings.

Several definitions of *yoga* are given in the *Bhagavad Gita* and *Patanjali's Yoga Sutras*, but all definitions of *yoga* are built around this *Law of Detachment* – that the one who is detached attracts, and the one who is attached repulses good energy.

The Sanskrit word *yoga* comes from the root "*yuj*," which means "to unite; to yoke." The first definition of *yoga* is "to become united" – "*samyoga*," whether you are united with God, with your own Self, or with the whole world. However, *yoga* may also mean the opposite, that is, "to be disunited, *viyoga*; to dissociate or sever your connection with pain or suffering" – "*duhkha-samyoga-viyogam yoga samjnitam*" (*Gita*. 6:23). So better not to go around saying that *yoga* only means "to unite." Another meaning of *yoga*, that Patanjali has given us, is restraint: "*Yogah citta vritti nirodhah*," "Yoga is restraining thought modification" (*Yoga Sutras*. 1:2). These then are the three general meanings of *yoga*: 1) to unite; 2) to disunite; and 3) to restrain – all leading to non-reaction and the underlying detachment.

One final definition of *yoga* which appears in the *Bhagavad Gita* is, "*Na ca mat-sthani bhutani / pasya me yoga aishvaram / bhuta-bhrn na ca bhuta-stho / mam'atma bhuta-bhavanah*" (*Gita*. 9:5) – the Lord says "Look at my creation; this is my *yoga*." Creative activity also is *yoga*. What is creative activity? Creative activity is an ability to create without becoming exhausted. The more you create, the more you are inspired.

Yoga and Detachment

According to Krishna, *duhkha* is a notion; suffering is a thought. Suffering has no substantiality because what gives suffering to one person gives joy to another. Take the notion of going to a lecture on Vedanta. Some people enjoy this kind of lecture and some people suffer through it, thinking. "When is this lecture going to end? Why did I walk into this hall?"

From the same situation, people harvest different experiences and results. Some people harvest joy, others garner pain. Hence, our *rishis* have concluded that suffering is relative, an interpretation, a thought, or an assumption. I *assume* that I am suffering, like one suffering in a dream. In your dream you have suddenly become a leprous beggar and you are crawling on the road, with oozing wounds all over your body, all your limbs being eaten away with the disease. As you slowly move along, hunger and thirst gnaw in your stomach. Someone throws a paper plate and you rush to grab that paper plate looking for something to eat. You find a few grains of cooked rice there and try to scrape them out. A dog leaps to get the paper plate, and then ... suddenly, you wake up! There you lay, in the comfort of your air-conditioned master bedroom! Now what? In a split second, all the suffering you experienced in your dream has simply vanished. Then you realize that you were dreaming that you were a beggar; all the details are simply a thought that you can easily set aside. Once you give up that thought, you realize your true glory and nature.

Therefore, Krishna says, "Suffering is only an interpretation." Give up that thought; stand apart from that assumption and be liberated. With a detached attitude, you renounce your pain. The lesson is: don't cooperate with your pain. For example, when you feel a headache in the morning, don't spend the rest of the day meditating on that headache, devoting all your attention and energy to rid yourself of the problem. You surf the internet to find how to alleviate your symptoms and, in the process, make a mountain out of a molehill. When you have a headache, don't let that thought control you. If you think, "I have a headache," even nature will echo you. "*Tathastu,*" "May it be so," because that is the thought you nourish.

Hence, this definition of *yoga* from Krishna: "*Yoga* is this ability to detach; the ability to stand apart," *samyoga viyogam*. Whatever is inconvenient to you, whatever gives you suffering or pain, step aside and observe it. When you detach and observe, objects lose their power over you. Only with your permission does thought gain power.

This principle is even true of relationships. People acquire enormous power over others – power that is borrowed from them. By way of your attachment, you lend them power. Attachment binds you and drags you like a tethered animal.

Therefore, Krishna says, "*duhkha-samyoga-viyogam yoga-samjnitam*" – *yoga* means renouncing your attachment to *duhkha* (*Gita*. 6:23). *Duhkha* is only a thought, only a dream, only an interpretation. Once we detach, we are free from all our suffering – like the famous story of Pingala, a woman in the *Bhagavatam*. Pingala pines away for someone who never comes, agonizing and suffering over and over again in her daydream about his arrival. Finally, one day, she decides, "It's only a thought," and from that point on her suffering ceases. She is liberated from her pain.

Just observe and don't cooperate with your suffering. Don't jump into identifying with what you experience. "Look before you leap," as the proverb says. Instead of assuming that you are suffering, observe it with a detached mind, like you are watching a movie, and find that there is no suffering at all!

Many things happen in a movie. For example, when the famous Indian actor, Amitabh Bacchan, plays the role of a coolie laden with heavy luggage, the whole audience feels sorry for the "poor man!" Then a cruel passenger puts one more bag on top, the audience cries and their tears start flowing and handkerchiefs come out of everyone's pockets. We cry watching this? Let me tell you a secret. While you pay for crying, Amitabh Bacchan is laughing, because his bank balance skyrockets 10 or 15 *lakhs*. You cry, he enjoys – isn't it all foolishness? Hence, watch and enjoy; the whole of life is a theatre. On various stages, many episodes unfold. Don't get attached. The first principle of *yoga* is, "*duhkha samyoga viyogam.*" "Be detached from your suffering."

Detachment, Pleasure and Bliss

Likewise, be detached from your pleasures. People want to detach from suffering by thinking of God and going to temples and seeking blessings. But, when pleasure comes, and the whole world is presented on a silver platter, you jump in spontaneous glee. But, even then, detachment is necessary, because when you indulge in pleasure, forgetting who you are, those pleasures later on entrap you. "*Ye hi samsparsa-ja bhoga / duhkha-yonaya eva te / ady-antavantah Kaunteya / na tesu ramate budhah*"

(*Gita*. 5:22). "Born of sense contacts, these pleasures are seeds of future pain." When you experience pleasure, be still and watch. When in pain, be calm and cool. Don't co-operate with either: don't self-forget and jump onto the Ferris wheel of pleasure and pain. Pleasure and pain move like "two halves of a wheel" – "*chakra vad vartante*." Pleasure goes up, pain comes down. Pain goes up, pleasure goes down." Life is a merciless wheel of pleasure and pain. Fall under the wheel and you will be run over and crushed. Step aside. Enjoy watching the wheel roll on and on. Detach and enjoy the whole movement; come to realize the true meaning of bliss!

Bliss does not come from attachment or indulgence. Attachment and indulgence only bring you pleasure and titillation. Eventually, that very pleasure will lead you to pain. When you detach from both pleasure and pain, you connect with Spirit and attain bliss. This is called "*atma sukha*." The other is called "*bhoga sukha*." One who enjoys this later *sukha* is called a "*bhogi*" – a consumer. The world encourages *bhogis* and the Spirit, *yogis*! That is why, today, we hear a great deal about consumerism, media encouraging consumption on one side and a disapproving backlash on the other.

Consumerism upholds the erroneous philosophy: "The more you indulge, the happier you become. Consuming *more* is the secret of happiness." It follows that the more chocolates you eat, the happier you will be. But our experience is that we enjoy the first chocolate. The second chocolate still brings some enjoyment. With a third, fourth or fifth chocolate pimples start popping out on your face. Once you finish the whole box, your stomach is aching, your appetite for nutritional food is lost, and you can't sleep at night due to the caffeine you've ingested.

From such experiences you learn that indulgence is not the way to happiness and true bliss. Scriptures advise, "Pain and pleasure will come of their own; detach and take only what is necessary." Thus the mind will purify and become subtle and sensitive. With detachment you access spiritual intelligence, true bliss. Life is full of joy.

Detachment is the secret and *Law of Happiness.* Anyone who is truly happy is a detached person. Yoga is *viyoga*, dis-uniting or detachment, stepping aside and watching.

Yoga and Pursuing Excellence

Another definition of *yoga*, according to Krishna, is "*yoga karmasu kaushalam*," "Pursuing a plan of action relentlessly to its end is *yoga*" (*Bhagavad Gita.* 2:50). Or another way of saying this is, "*Yoga* is pursuing excellence in work." Doing this, you have to gather your attention from other distracting and dissipating pursuits and concentrate on one particular work.

Look at cricket stars or sportsmen in general. They each pursue excellence in their own field. Observe how much discipline they have! They must adopt regular habits. They cannot eat "junk food," must go to sleep early, and forego watching late night television. They cannot entertain any other pursuits while they are training. Because they are pursuing excellence, they develop rigorous self-discipline.

Such people also have a certain detachment. Suppose that tomorrow is a cricket match. Today all the players are indulging in watching movies, drinking and dancing until 4 o'clock in the morning. The match is to begin at 7 a.m. sharp. Will they be able to perform? They cannot. Pursuing something relentlessly imposes certain disciplines. Your girl friend may call on the phone. But you reproach her, saying, "Don't distract me. I have to focus on my training program." Once you are fascinated with a goal, nothing can distract you. Hence, Krishna says, "*Yoga karmasu kaushalam,*" "Relentless pursuit of a goal is called *yoga.*"

These days, youngsters want to look slim, because, presently, beauty is defined by slenderness. If you look like a dry twig, then you are beautiful. If you are a little plump, you are considered ugly. Some people believe it – after all, beauty is a perception. What is beautiful for you may be unbecoming for another.

A young girl wants to look beautiful, so she fasts for three days a week – no potato chips, no ice cream, no chocolates or soda pops, only salads, morning and evening. She drinks eight glasses of pure water everyday, avoiding even tender coconut water because it is highly saturated with sugar. Looking like a twig, she moves about thinking that she is beautiful. Since she thinks she is beautiful, everyone else also thinks that she is beautiful. What you think, others also think. You send those messages out and everyone picks them up. By this kind of discipline, she convinces herself that she is beautiful. The poor thing starves herself – but for the sake of an ideal, her dream! Although we may not ourselves advocate this particular goal personally, look at what effort she is making and self-discipline she is developing. She, too, is pursuing an ideal, and sacrifice, detachment and concentration are involved. In this example, Krishna's definition of detachment is explicit: "Pursuing excellence in work is *yoga*."

Obstacles to Excellence

Both definitions of *yoga* are built around the *Law of Detachment*. The first is to detach from *duhkha* or suffering. Our problem is that we have a special seductive, suicidal fascination for our *duhkha*. When you sit alone in your meditation room, what do you think about? You are supposed to be chanting, "Rama, Rama," and thinking about the beauty, glory and the visage of Lord Rama. But what are you thinking about? Raman Nair, who borrowed some money from you and never paid you back, and how you want to break his neck. Or perhaps you are reviewing in your mind the heaps of insults others piled upon you over a lifetime.

We have a special fascination for our own misery. Like a pimple on your face – you want the pimple to go away, but what do you do? Constantly thinking about it, every half hour you run into the bathroom, look in the mirror and poke at the pimple until finally it breaks open. Your behavior and reaction to the circumstance is very ironic. What we want to avoid, we trail behind.

What is necessary is not to "fall in love" with your suffering. Don't promote and brood and give all your attention to your suffering. Give you attention to something wonderful and beautiful. Although this *Law of Yoga* is very important, we are generally unable to put that *Law* into practice. Just give up this idea that you are unhappy, dissociate from it. Think that you are happy. When you think this way, happiness spontaneously happens. The whole of nature will support you. What you think, you become. "*Yoga karmasu kausalam*." "Forget your misery and relentlessly pursue excellence." That is *yoga*.

Yoga as Non-Reaction

Now we come to another definition of *yoga* is "*samatvam yoga ucyate*" (*Gita*. 2:48). *Yoga* means "equanimity of mind," "non-reaction under pressure." You may be suffering, or ill, or in the midst of a dilemma, like Bhishma, lying on the bed of arrows;

Lord Krishna's advice is, "Keep your dignity and don't react." Bhishma remained dignified in the face of death and did not cry. He was not thinking of suffering and the arrows that penetrated his body. Instead, he remained focused upon the immortal life, the Self, *Brahman*. These arrows were only flowers for him. Bhishma gives us a prime example of "*samatvam yoga ucayte*" (*Gita*. 2:48). "Non-reaction to situations is *yoga*." Keep a serene frame of mind, a calm cool mind. Youngsters often say, "Be cool, man; be cool." Ramakrishna also talked about inner coolness. A balanced person will be cool inside.

Once, a parent brought his son to me and implored, "Swamiji, my son is a little upset over something and doesn't confide in me. Please talk to him." So the young man and I met. He drove me around in his car while we chatted, then he dropped me off at my residence, and he returned home. When he met his father, the boy reported, "The *Swami* is cool!" A *swami* is supposed to be cool! Teenagers' expression, "Be cool," has deep meaning.

Be cool; don't get excited by success or failure. That coolness of mind, the ability of non-reaction constitutes emotional intelligence or "*samatvam*." We must gain a certain control over our emotions.

Ordinary intelligence is analytical. We tend to be fascinated with analytical intelligence, looking into a situation, reviewing all the factors involved, analyzing the data and offering a solution. That technical and analytical intelligence may help us tackle the outside world of objects – but you also need emotional intelligence, the means to handle the inner world of emotion and thought. Unfortunately that emotional intelligence is rarely promoted.

Many highly qualified people are very poor in the management of their emotions. They shout, scream, fret, fume and swear, with no control whatsoever over their emotions. The management of your emotions is important as a complement to your technical and analytical skills. Without emotional intelligence others will despise you, and your analytic and technical skills will become burdensome, joyless effort.

Emotional intelligence means "a balanced mind." *Yoga* means both skill in action and equanimity of mind ("*yoga karmasu kaushalam,*" and "*samatvam yoga ucyate*"). We have to activate and demonstrate our equanimity *while* we are engaged in worldly pursuits. Practice equanimity in the company of your family, your children and your enemies, as well as in success and failure.

Non-Reaction in Practice

Don't think that the Himalayan caves are the only place where one can practice equanimity. You may live for 20 years in the Himalayan caves and never shout once, never use any harsh words or never even think a negative thought. You envision yourself as an accomplished *yogi*! That's because in the mountains there is nobody to shout at, nobody to provoke you, so you have an "apparent" sense of equanimity and pride yourself in having attained emotional balance. But, when you walk down from the mountain into the city of Rishikesh and are challenged by someone who pokes fun at your appearance, the same old divisive person emerges again. Your so-called inner peace – promoted and induced solely by the serene and isolated Himalayan environment – is a very shallow peace. But in an interactive environment, when people abuse and shout at you or look down upon you, can you keep your calm? *Yoga* is non-reaction to these various phenomenological experiences.

At the same time, non-reaction does not mean you ignore or fail to respond to situations. Some people parrot, "Swamiji said, 'practice non-reaction,' so if anything goes wrong, I temporarily become like a stone." Then, after the class, you ride back home on a crowded bus. You hang onto the beam and just then, a hefty, big booted man enters the bus, slips just ahead of you and accidentally stomps on your toe. Your toes are crushed, but suddenly you remember that Swamiji said, "Don't react." While trying to repress and swallow the pain, tears well up in your eyes. You clear your throat loudly to give the man a hint that he is stepping on your toes. You can hardly breathe. You hum to yourself, "Don't react; don't react." Later on, when you are with your friends, you blurt out the whole story, including how you "didn't react"!

That is not what is meant by non-reaction! This type of response is a misapplication of non-reaction. An appropriate response is called for. Tell him, "Sir, you are stepping on my toes! Kindly move your foot." Anyone will happily respond and apologize, too. Non-reaction means to respond but not to react. Recognize the difference between these two ways of interacting with the world.

Another way of reacting is to become so angry that you give the man a punch in the nose. Unfortunately, you forgot to check out his size and profession before you let loose with your punch, and he happened to be the Police Commissioner! He uses his cell phone to summon his subordinates and they bodily carry you off to the police station. There you will get back what you gave to him, with compound interest! The following day you are kicked out and dropped on the road, broken, belittled and bent out of shape. Such are the consequences of over-reaction. Our minds swing between the two extremes – passivity and inaction or anger and over-reaction. Neither of these responses is what is meant by non-reaction. Non-reaction evolves out of practice and a balanced mind.

Fine-Tuning our Responses and Sustaining Success

Like a musical instrument, our minds are capable of fine-tuning. If the strings of a musical instrument are too tight, it cannot produce melodious, harmonizing sounds. If the strings are too loose, there is only noise and no music. The meaning of non-reaction is to fine-tune your responses to suit the situation. Animals react immediately. If I step on the tail of a dog, the dog will turn immediately around and bark – or even bite! But the human is capable of processing sensation and information, taking time, choosing an appropriate response and then expressing or executing that response.

Some people process well, but they don't perform well. When we say non-reaction, it does not mean absolute non-reaction, inaction and passivity, rather, it means *choosing* a response appropriate to the situation. Reaction and response are different. The *yogi's* power is one of responding appropriately.

A detached person can organize his or her energies and channel those energies for the purpose of realizing the intermittent and/or life goals they have set. Some people think that a *yogi* should exist without any goals, floating like a dry leaf in the wind and the storm. *Yoga* does not mean that you have no life goals. *Yoga* means, "Have goals in life and pursue those goals, but if you don't fulfill them, then respond appropriately; don't react." If you react, you will be unable to learn from your mistakes or to improve upon your successes.

Sometimes one success is enough and we become egoistic and go around bragging, "Do you know who I am?" "Do you know what I did?" Take, for example, a politician who wins a landslide victory in an earlier election and then, thinking that he has made it to the "top" and his task is done, forgets about meeting with and listening to his constituency. He assumes, "I have them all in my hand; what do I care?" He travels first class, meets other important people but ignores the grassroots work. Because this one victory has gone to his head, he loses the next election.

If you want to have sustained success, victory after victory, then detach from your past successes. If you are attached to previous successes, you will not be motivated to attain further success. Detachment from our prior successes is vital to continuous achievement. So, too, is detachment from failure.

Some people fail in one attempt and then acquire a defeatist attitude thinking that they are forever Mr. or Ms. Failure. For example, a high school student fails in one college entrance exam and his or her self-perception changes, affecting all his or her future exams. Thereafter, whatever challenge he or she undertakes is tainted by an attitude of self-doubt. This attitude ensures a self-fulfilling prophecy. After one failure why do you condemn yourself as a complete failure?

Sometimes, even before their exams have begun, certain teenagers already have made the assumption that they will fail. They have already drawn a conclusion without any foundation other than their fear and self-doubt. With that attitude, they take the exam and indeed fail. Then the teenager runs to his parents, crying, "Didn't I tell you it would end up this way?"

One failure doesn't make you a complete failure. In fact, failures are stepping-stones to success. Neither failure nor success should go to your head, because from failure you learn, and despite any success you can still improve. There is no final success in this world; your efforts must go on and on. That is the meaning of non-reaction.

Restraint is Yoga

In his *Yoga Sutras*, Patanjali (the master of *yoga*) defines *yoga* as "*Yogah citta vritti nirodhah*" (1:2). "*Yoga* is restraining thought modification." *Yoga* is an ability to control your thoughts. Most of the people have little or no control over their thoughts. They alternate between depressed and excited thoughts – like maniac depressive personality disorder. Sometimes your friend is on top of the world and, when he speaks with you, he vows to help you with a big project. Then, the following week, when you approach about his promise, he boils over, shouts curses at you, and slams the door in your face.

Some people experience swings of excitement and depression. Depression decreases one's energy, and excitement dissipates one's energy. Emotional turbulence and error are fostered by such violent swings. Sometimes we are very angry and other times very nice – like Dr. Jekyll and Mr. Hyde syndrome – everyone's friend by day, but a monster by night. Who can reconcile these two disparate personalities? A split personality is fostered by alternating hypocritical and hysteric responses.

Patanjali says you can control these violent moods and energy. It is neither difficult, nor do you need medication and psychiatric treatment for this. By exercising self-discipline you can establish control. Some people claim that such extremes in behavior are all body chemistry and that one's temperament is not within the bounds of personal control. "I am diabetic and my sugar fluctuates; that's why I become angry." Modern doctors tell us that we possess will power and that through meditation the brain can produce neuro-peptides. These energies are released and the neuro-peptide messengers travel all over the body's nervous system, upgrading one's immunity and energy level. All that is required is that you send a message. Since you have the necessary will power, use it, and change the very chemistry of your body! Will it, and it shall be done! Utilizing will, even mountains can be moved.

We are not helpless victims of the moods of our minds. We can command a mood and dismiss a mood, provided that we understand that there is something deeper in us. We have the service of your neurological system at hand. If we have the detachment to stand apart from our thoughts and moods and emotions, we will be better equipped to organize our behavior.

Moods have great energy. Even to swing to the lowest level of depression, thought energy is required. But, most of the time, these energies are out of control. Use your will positively for realization of your goals.

Patanjali's *Yoga Sutras* also tell us that it is possible to restrain our minds and organize our powerful, inborn, psychic energy. Our minds are not limited mechanical energy. For example, a car engine allows a vehicle to travel at a certain speed and utilizes fuel which is limited to the size of the gas tank. By contrast, the human range is very vast. Either a Buddha or a *buddhu* (a fool) can be fashioned from the same human being. Such magic is impossible for an ordinary machine. A car will perform even if you shout at it, spit on it or dent it in anger. But, if you spit on the waiter at the restaurant and angrily demand, "Get me a glass of water," he will bring a glass of cold water and pour it over your head! You can choose to be more cordial and artfully suggest, "I'll increase your tip by fifty cents, if you bring me a large glass of cold water," and the waiter will be motivated to offer his best service.

You can de-motivate or inspire a human being but not a machine. Once this is firmly understood, you will strive to control and manage your moods and emotions better. But, however much you can inspire another person, the greatest inspiration is self-inspiration – to "lift yourself by your own bootstraps." That is *yoga*. For that, you require detachment. If you are attached to your little pleasures and pains, you will never achieve that miracle of transforming yourself into your potential, your "fullness." For that, detachment – self-control over your moods and whims – is basic.

Now, the question arises: How do I restrain my emotions and mind? "*Yogah citta vritti nirodhah.*" How do you use detachment to control all the mind's passions and various levels of energy? First understand that when you detach you gain power, and when you are attached, you lose power. Attachment creates lot of negative energy. For example, you are attached to your granddaughter and will indulge her with anything. When she asks for a soda pop, you bring it, even if you have to go to several stores to find the right brand. Once your granddaughter understands your attachment, she can twist you by the tail and extract anything she wants. However, when you are detached, you have control. When you have no control, you indulge either yourself or others.

Mind's Moods and Modes

The six moods of the mind are: *muda, vimuda, kshipta, vikshipta, ekagra, nirodha* – that is, dull, extremely dull, distracted, extremely distracted, one-pointed and controlled. Sometimes you are in a dull or a disinterested state of mind (*muda*), or in an agitated state of mind when you claim to have no control over your emotions (*kshipta*). "*Citta kapi*" – "mind is like a monkey." There is a saying about the mind: "*Markadasya surapanam, ma-dhey vrichika damsanam tato paribhutavesam.*" If an ordinary monkey cannot sit still, imagine a "drunken monkey stung by a scorpion and haunted by a ghost." That is our general state of our mind. Unless one controls the mind, he or she will not be able to realize their potential. How do you control the mind? A story from the *Ramayana* about how Rama defeated the Monkey King, Vali, provides an illustration.

The mind is like Vali, this Monkey King, who sucks half the power of anyone that happens to come in front him – the very reason why Rama avoided coming into Vali's purview. If Rama had, Vali would definitely have been victorious over Rama. So Rama hid himself behind the tree where Vali could not see him, watched carefully, took aim and then hit Vali with an arrow.

We ought to deal similarly with the mind. Don't struggle with the mind. Just observe the mind and all its fluctuations. When you fight with the mind, the mind overpowers you. If you fight with the mind directly, it gains power over you; if you observe the mind, you gain power over your mind. The *Bhagavad Gita* says, "*Prakasam ca pravrttim ca / moham eva ca Pandava / na dvesti sampravrttani na nivrttani kanksati* " (14:22). "Whether your mind has a peaceful disposition, agitated disposition, or a dull and malicious disposition, one neither hates nor loves its peacefulness, agitation or dullness." One learns not to fight with the mind.

On Restraining the Mind

I am reminded of another famous story. Once, a bald man wanted to grow hair. Even now, people spend millions trying to overcome baldness. Rather, they should save their money and enjoy their baldness! Baldness is a sign of wisdom. God does not give bountiful hair and brains together. A hairy person will have no brain, and a brainy person will have no hair – because all his hair has become gray matter! As your intelligence grows, the hair disappears. All great men were bald – Gandhi, Nehru, Churchill, Patel. What is there to be ashamed of in baldness other than one's petty pride?

So the bald man, the main character of this story, commissioned a great physician who claimed to be able to cure his baldness within five days. He prescribed the bald man to take this hair oil and apply it everyday for a week." As he was leaving the doctor's office, the doctor added, "I forgot to tell you one other condition; when you apply the oil, don't think of eggs." The bald man said, "Oh, that's very easy. I'm a vegetarian. I have never taken eggs." Then, the following day, when the bald man took the oil in his palm and applied it to his head, he reminisced, "What was it that I was not supposed to think about? Oh, yes. An egg." After remembering, all he could think of and visualize in his mind's eye was, "Egg, egg, egg" – like a *mantra*. The poor man, every time he looked in the mirror, all he could think was a bald, white egg! Earlier, he had never thought of an egg. Now the thought of an egg preoccupied his mind.

The moral is that, if you fight with the mind, you will be the loser. The best way to control the mind is to apply restraint

– wait, have patience and watch. Of course, you can change your food habits a little; you can change the books you read. All those secondary support systems are advisable, but the final purification of the mind is to detach and observe. In a detached state, allow the mind to flow. This is how we learn to purify our minds and control our responses.

Purifying the Mind

There is a famous story about the Buddha and Ananda, his disciple. They were roaming about the villages of Bihar. Now, Buddha and Ananda, passed by a pool of water and then walked a little further into a village. Somewhere beyond the village, along the road, Buddha was feeling thirsty and asked, "Ananda, I'm thirsty. Can you please fetch some water for me?" Ananda went back to the little pool to obtain the water, but unfortunately, because a few bullock carts passed that river, the pool of water had become muddied and undrinkable. Ananda moaned, "What will I do now? Let me try to clean up this pool of water." He jumped into the pool and started plucking out all the rotten leaves and fallen twigs, but the more he tried, the more muddied the water became. He struggled for several hours until finally he gave up. He just could not get the water clean.

Disappointed, he returned to the Buddha and said, "Lord, I tried my best to clear the water and bring you something to drink, but when I tried, the water became more and more muddied. Finally, having failed in my mission, I gave up." Buddha replied, "Actually, I wasn't thirsty. I just wanted to teach you a lesson: If you want to clean up a pool of water, don't jump into it. Just sit on the banks of the pool and the water will clear itself. All the muck will settle down and clear water will surface."

Similarly, if you want to clear up the mind and you fight with it, the mind becomes more and more unclean. When you don't struggle with your emotions, trying to suppress them, and instead just watch them, the same poison that the mind contained organizes itself into nectar. This is the miracle of detachment. The same energy that creates conflict, suspicion, anger, jealousy and envy, transforms itself and becomes very positive, loving energy. You don't have to do anything. That is a fundamental *Law of Detachment*. When we observe the mind, the energy of conflict transforms into harmony and love.

Solving Emotional Problems

In your daily life, suppose you have an emotional problem with your family – not a technical problem, like how to build a house. That you can discuss with your family any time, but an emotional problem is more difficult to discuss with those immediately involved. Here is a hint: emotional problems can rarely be solved by direct confrontation, analysis or discussion.

Like a guerilla warrior, they hide behind some tree or crevice, shooting at you. Emotional problems must simply be forgotten! Don't make them the focus of your discussion. If you discuss emotional problems, the more they will occupy and confuse your mind. Soon, you will start rationalizing, finding logical answers to explain your position. Then your position becomes very rigid, and you turn the whole household into a war zone.

The best thing is to just forget it. Refuse to carry emotions forward. If someone calls you a donkey, forget it. Don't dredge and re-dredge the incident up by calling him or her some other name. Forget it. That is detachment, and the only way to solve emotional problems! Patanjali says, "If you want to handle the mind, detach. Don't fight with the mind. If you are angry, be angry; if you are jealous, be jealous - but remain detached! The more you fight, the more you become its victim." Mind will drag you more and more into the mire of emotions.

The mind has intelligence; you have only to watch, especially in the case of strong emotions like jealousy. Don't repeat negative thoughts and images in your mind, for example, "I am jealous, I'm not sure what to do, but I want to control my jealousy. I want to take charge of my emotions." The more you try to control your emotions, the more of a hypocrite you will become, pretending to be a good person. Replace your negative thoughts with something positive. You may even offer a kind gesture to your enemy, perhaps giving a flower, though, in fact, you wanted to break his or her neck! Even mentally offering a flower will do. Otherwise you may exhaust all the flowers in your garden and the flower market. Superficial changes do not alter a rotten core. The best way to deal with emotions is to stand apart, detached.

The *Bhagavad Gita* offers this advice: "*Guna gunesu vartanta*;" "Your emotions are a play of the *gunas*" (3:28). Never attach; rather step aside and observe. Then watch the miracle of nectar being made out of poison, emotions organizing themselves. Therefore Patanjali tells us, "*Yogah citta vritti nirodhah / tada drastuh svarupe 'vasthanam*" – "When you watch the mind, the mind organizes and quiets itself" (*Yoga Sutras*. 1:2-3). You don't have to intervene. Through detachment, the mind will organize itself. As a result of watching, you are able to abide in your Self (*svarupa*).

Losing the Battle

Earlier you were fighting with your mind and dissipating your energy as a result. An extroverted person has little time to listen to the inner whispering of eternity. When you no longer fight the mind, you have the inner leisure to listen to the musing and whispering of Spirit, the voice of the soul. "Those who are attached are bound by their thoughts": "*Vritti sarupyam itaratra*" (*Yoga Sutras*. 1:4). As you fight with your enemy, some of the qualities of the opponent also come to abide in you. So, too, if you fight with the mind, you become one with the mind you oppose. Even if he is a criminal, you may imagine, "He is very famous. I want to be like him," the values and the virtues you have been fighting for are lost!

Say, for example, a dictatorship attacks a democratic country, and the later stands ready to protect its values. Ironically, the first thing the democratic government does is to suspend all the rights of its citizens! Once these rights are suspended, there is nothing left for which to fight! The whole purpose was to protect the freedom of your citizens from the enemy. That is why the country exists as a sovereign nation and strives to defend its borders and lifestyle. But in its attempt to fight the enemy, that democracy also imbibes and cultivates some of its enemy's values. Finally, no distinction exists between one's self and one's enemy; you are as bad (or as good) as each other. The rise and death of your fight with evil is complete. After that your battle has no sustaining value. Only the same trading of abuses, crossfire and bombing goes on. Both sides have found their level and are equal. The good man and the bad man inhabit the same zone of moral ambiguity.

A virtuous person has a double responsibility. He must fight against evil – but without becoming evil! For that, one requires an attitude of detachment. This detached attitude empowers you to handle life in a much better way.

Detachment is Supreme

As far as mind is concerned, detachment is the *mantra*. There is no other way to control or manage the mind. Don't judge or suppress the mind. If you judge the mind, it will rebel. When someone calls you a hurtful name or judges you, what do you do? Someone calls you an "evil person," and you become so desperate that your mind twirls and spins with thoughts of revenge. Finally admit, "Yes, I am evil." So what? Under stress you fall into the suggestive trap of your detractor. Just watch. Remain detached. Detachment has the greatest force and its power is infinite.

Understand the situation and then orchestrate the right responses. With that quality of mind, nurturing and practicing detachment, you will be able to do as Patanjali says, "*Tada drastuh svarupe 'vasthanam*" (*Yoga Sutras*. 1:3). "You will be able to access the Infinite Intelligence of Spirit."

Yoga means pursuing excellence, keeping your mind in balance and attaining access to Spirit as a result. Once these qualities are yours, then you are a *yogi*. Even while you are driving, you can enjoy the power of *yoga*. Concentrating on your driving, your mind is in a quiet state of non-reaction. When another car jumps out in front and overtakes your car, you don't react. You only bring out the right response and, in the process, access the Spirit. As a result, Spiritual Intelligence manifests through your choice-making activities and lends its power in all that you do. All your activities become a channel for spiritual unfoldment – a dynamic *yoga* and true meditation. You need not close your eyes thinking only that type of meditation is *yoga*. Closing the eyes to meditate is not *yoga*. You must have insight into Spirit, and for that the mind has to be calm. Don't try to quiet the mind directly. It doesn't and won't happen. Instead, concentrate upon a program of action.

Some people tell me, "Swamiji, I'm going to take one day a week off from my work in order to learn to quiet my mind." That way you will never calm the mind, but you may get a good nap! To attain mental quietude, pursue a course of action. While you are pursuing the action, don't react, only do the right thing. That is quietude of the mind. *Yoga* requires a supremely active person. That person alone attains absolute mental quietude and, in that process, invokes the Infinite Power of Spirit. His or her actions are aglow in the light of Spirit, and whatever he or she touches becomes a success. This is the true meaning of detachment and *yoga*.

Invoking Intelligence

Through the *yoga* of detachment, you accomplish three levels of intelligence. Level one is the pursuit of excellence. The second level is your ability to keep your mind calm under all circumstances, gathering no stress while actively engaged in life. The third level is that of accessing the Spirit. These three levels we may alternately call: 1) analytical and/or technical intelligence; 2) emotional intelligence; and, 3) spiritual intelligence. These three levels of intelligence are to be invoked while engaged in your daily activities and projects.

Mere analytical and/or technical intelligence is not enough. This level of development will only make you a sick, hypocritical person. Even if you are very effective, you will have no sustained friendships, others will talk behind your back and shower blame upon you. Such a person, himself, will curse and blame everyone claiming, "No one else works. I am the only achiever."

By invoking all three levels of intelligence, you enjoy success, peace and happiness. Otherwise you may be successful, but without peace and happiness of what use is success? Living like a silk worm, you produce silk and cover yourself with silk. Although you glisten in the sunlight, what is your fate? The Sericulturist comes, picks you up, drops you into boiling water, takes the silk, and you are dead!

Detachment is the key to activating all levels of intelligence. *Yoga* means detaching from your pain and pleasure, keeping a cool frame of mind, choosing appropriate responses to situations, and pursuing excellence relentlessly such that nothing can distract you from your chosen path. With that kind of detachment, we can all become *yogis*. Then alone do you live life in the true spirit of *yoga*, truly detached and capable of experiencing the ecstasy of unconditionally loving all. Apply this law. Be detached and find your fulfillment.

Seven

The Spiritual Law of Leela

The Playful Flow

The seventh and final Hindu Spiritual Law to be discussed is the *Law of Leela*, the *Law of Playfulness* or the *Law of Least Effort*. The whole nature is organized on this *Law of Leela* or *Playfulness*. Nature is very playful. Children are very playful because they are very close to nature. When we grow up, we move away from nature and become crooked calling it "worldly wisdom." Children's wisdom is of a different sort. They go to the seashore, take wet sand, pack it around their feet, and make little caves – as if they are reliving some ancient past. We emerged from caves and now children want to return to the caves. Then they put little pebbles inside the cave and say, "This is a cow. This is a bull. This is a cat," etc., and they play for hours like that. When they tire, they smash the whole sand village and go away. With the same foot with which they created the playful scene, they destroy it.

Children also talk to nature's creatures, like the butterflies: "Come here. I want to catch you." The butterfly darts here and there, and children run after it for some time and then suddenly forget about it. This is *leela*.

Children bring a lot of mirth into their lives *and* into our lives, also! If there is a child at home, we also feel young. Without a child in the home, we feel prematurely old. Children bring a quality of playfulness and effortlessness wherever they go. They can dance and prance and play in the sun. Meanwhile, we worry, "Oh, my child must be feeling hungry. He has not eaten since the morning," but the child has no problem. Children are very innocent. Their energy flows. Children are the perfect example of the flow experience. They can maneuver around and be with anyone. For example, if you tell the child, "Don't go to the neighbor's house; he's not our friend," when the child goes there, he will say, "Mummy says you are not our friend," and mummy is very embarrassed. A child creates new energy. The child experiences this spontaneous and continuous outpouring of fresh energy.

As we grow up, we lose that capacity. Blocks develop in our personality – jealousy, fear, greed and intolerance. Due to these blocks, our energies fail to find their natural outlet and expression, and we become ill. That is the reason behind sickness. By the age of 45, we have all kinds of illnesses, because we don't generate the flow experience. We don't grow; we don't learn; we are worried and serious, rather than playful. We are neither caring, nor sharing, nor loving. We cannot look at the stars and wonder. Instead we constantly gaze into our own little problems and become enclosed in that suffocating atmosphere. We forget to look through the window and see the beautiful moonrise. We leave no time to feel the wind, caress the flowers that dance in the breeze. We are so enclosed in our own petty selves that we find it very difficult to break out of it and experience "the flow." Our energies are blocked and, consequently, we are ill.

Nature does things very effortlessly. Nature follows this *Law of Effortless Ease* and accomplishes all of its activities in that manner, not wasting any energy at all! Therefore, playfulness, effortless ease and creativity, all mean the same thing.

Effortlessness

Some days your mind is very clear; everything blooms around you, and you work effortlessly. In modern terminology, such states of consciousness are called the "flow." No hindrance whatsoever appears – a state of playfulness abounds, an effortless, moving state of creativity. When you are in that flow, whatever you do becomes creative. When these energies cease to flow, then what you do may even become destructive. Even if you do the right thing, others misunderstand. In that state you may read the newspaper from beginning to end, but nothing is clear to you.

The Law of Playfulness says: "Maximum achievement is possible with minimum effort," meaning that creativity is the quotient of achievement divided by effort. For example, if your achievement is 10 units and your effort is 20 units, your creativity is only .5. If your achievement is 10 units and your effort is only 5 units, your creativity is +2, meaning that the achievement of very creative people is maximal and their effort minimal. A situation comes that without any effort at all you achieve. That effortless state is playfulness or *leela*.

Once someone asked Picasso (the world-famous, 20th-century European artist) to draw a circle. Ordinarily, we draw circles using a compass and making it turn one complete round with both the point and pencil applied to the paper. You may even draw a circle, without the use of an instrument, but it will not be properly formed. Picasso took his pencil, made a quick movement and formed the most perfect circle. Drawing is a most effortless, creative experience for someone of great expertise. If an expert dancer comes onto a stage, she instantly breaks into the dance. Thereafter, she does not consciously attend to what she is doing. Her dance is effortless and may go on for hours. If we try to imitate her, sure enough, we will suffer from disjointed limbs – but not her.

Similarly, the planets "dance" around the sun – by itself a most difficult effort. The earth has been going round itself in a somersault-like motion, and also rotating around the sun for countless years, making no noise, no protest or complaint, and getting no rest at all! Imagine doing the traditional *parikrama* around an Indian temple like that! One round and you will say, "That's enough for me," sit down on the nearest step and wait until your dizziness subsides. For two days you lie in bed! Suppose the earth decided to rest, and stopped its activities; the whole universe would come to a grinding halt. Everything is well orchestrated and timed. Every planet – indeed, everyone – should flow with ease in his or her own trajectory. If one breaks the flow, then problems begin.

The river also flows effortlessly, coming down from the high mountaintops, gradually moving towards its destination. Huge rocks may come in the way of the river, but the river flows backward momentarily, and then again "finds" its way around, under or over the rock, eventually wearing the rock down to silt! Whatever the case, the river does not complain, "Everyone creates obstacles for me. Nobody likes me. Who put all these rocks in the way?" The river always finds its way forward. When you or I face obstacles in trying to achieve our goals, we complain, "Nobody in this organization allows me to get my work done the way it ought to be! Everyone puts obstacles in my path."

We fail to follow the *Law of Least Effort*, the way of spontaneity and creativity. No one creates obstacles for you – provided that you continue moving forward, making your effort towards your goal. The river sustains constant movement never taking any rest until its oceanic destination is reached. It is a flow experience. The river makes no effort at all.

In the case of a tree, water is constantly being pumped

upwards and transpires through the leaves. There are scientific demonstrations which show how quickly the water flows through a tree and evaporates. Does the tree make any noise when the water is pumped up its trunk and branches? Millions of gallons of water are constantly flowing upward, and still there is no noise at all.

God has created your digestive system, making it possible to swallow food: "*Aham vaisvanaro bhutva / praninam deham asritah / pran'apana-samayuktah / pacamyannam catur-vidham*" (*Gita*. 15:14) "I abide in the body of all beings in the form of digestive fire, controlling in-going and out-going breath, and digest the four-fold food." What a perfect system! When you swallow the food, the food must first move across the windpipe and then into the esophagus. When you swallow food, it may accidentally fall into your windpipe. However, God has created a remarkable arrangement. A little flap comes over the windpipe, so that when food negotiates across this region, it slips over the flap and into the esophagus. Because of the peristaltic movement, the food goes down properly, and reaches the stomach. Various enzymes flow into the stomach, and food is digested. Is there any noise? Only when you eat wrong kind of food! But that's your problem, not God's! If you eat the right kind of food, the right quantity at the right time, and with the right attitude, then there will be no noise at all. Food is digested properly and the unnecessary acid and gas will not be produced. What perfection! Does the stomach take any leave? It goes on and on performing its task. The heart functions constantly. So, too, the lungs – and without rest!

Minimum Effort, Maximum Achievement

Creativity means rest-less activity; no rest is necessary. A creative person is always active and never complains. Such a person is always inspired. The more we act, the more inspired we are. The more we function, the more flow we experience. And the more flow we experience, the more we are inspired. The best way to inspire, to bring out your inner energy, is to work unceasingly and enjoy your work. When you work unceasingly, and you experience that flow of energy, work becomes a spontaneous, playful, joyful experience. According to this law, the most intelligent person is the most effortless person. Intelligence is equated with effortlessness. Effortless creativity and maximum output from minimum energy go hand in hand.

Once I locked myself out of my room, leaving my key inside. This automatic lock took hold when the door was pulled shut. Now, how to retrieve the key that is inside? I looked around and thought that I might have to break the door open. That is certainly a cumbersome and expensive way of opening the door, requiring a lot of effort! Next, I thought, "Why not call the locksmith?" The locksmith came, saw the problem and said, "Oh, this is a big job. I have to cut the lock. It will cost you 500 rupees." In relief, I hastily agreed, "Any amount is fine, because I have to get inside again."

Then, through the latticed window, the locksmith happened to see that the key was lying just inside on a table. He took a small magnet, tied it to the end of the stick, and stretched the stick through the window. The key clung to the magnet, the locksmith withdrew the apparatus, and handed me the key! Within one minute the problem was solved! Then I objected, "For this you want me to pay 500 rupees?" He replied, "Swami, you cannot change your word. You said 500 rupees for the job!" I paid him for his intelligence, not for the amount of effort! His effort consisted of very little. But his ingenuity, intelligence and experience – saving me the cost of a new door – was worth far more than I spent. I paid him, and he left contented.

On some other occasion, I again locked myself out of my room. So, I phoned someone who posed this simple (and ironic) question, "Do you have a credit card?" Someone produced a credit card, ran it by the lock, and, surprisingly, the door opened. Again, it was very effortless.

Such stories remind us to spend some time to think, evaluate the situation, and activate your intelligence. There is always an *upaya* (an effortless means) for doing things, a least expensive way of doing things. But we must spend some time thinking. Instead of immediately jumping into the fray with our mind panicking, just be calm and take stock. Find the *upaya* – the shortest distance between two points – and solve the problem.

When you walk the straight line, you reach the other point easily. Any other way you walk will take longer and require more energy. Evaluate the situation, activate your intuitive and spiritual powers and arrive at the solution. This is what we call spontaneity.

Spontaneity is not simply an analytical or frenetic or agitated response. Whenever a problem comes we immediately think, "Oh, what will I do? What will happen to me if I don't solve this problem? What planet has turned against me?" Why is this happening to me?" All irrelevant issues come to the surface. "Why is God against me? Why does God favor my neighbor?" Instead, why not look at the issue with a calm, quiet mind? Without a serene mind, you end up spending a lot of energy and achieving very little.

I am reminded of the example of Alexander the Great in applying this *Law of Least Effort.* Once, when Alexander the Great was a boy, he was asked to make an egg stand on its tip. Everyone was trying every which way, but no one could succeed. At last, Alexander was called. He took the egg and put slight pressure on it. The eggshell cracked slightly without breaking the skin that lined the inner liquid, and the egg stood on its tip without difficulty. Anyone could have done the same thing, but this novel approach did not strike anyone. This is what I call effortless ease. This method of problem solving – using the least effort – is the most intelligent approach.

Prayatna: *Adequate and Appropriate Effort*

An intelligent person is one who spends least energy, attains maximum achievement, and, in the process, creates a better life for himself and others. You must be patient in employing this law. There is an effortless method (an *upaya*) to solve any problem. The knack of effortlessness is due to *prayatna* (adequate effort), not in simply *yatna*. *Yatna* means just "effort" *Prayatna* means "adequate and appropriate effort."

For example, farmers in India work hard and toil from morning until evening every day throughout the year. But what is their productivity? Very little, because they don't use the most effective techniques! *Upaya* is a necessary ingredient in creativity. Using your intelligence you can go about your work playfully and accomplishments as well as miracles will happen. Make it a principle in life. If you put forth relaxed effort, the outcome will be better. Often, when you apply frenetic effort, the outcome will be minimal.

The outcome of any effort depends upon the *way* effort is applied. When America handled the Taliban problem, they quietly analyzed the data, took stock of the world situation, created a global coalition, marshaled their resources and army, and then went about their work. If they had immediately bombed Afghanistan, they would have created a problem. In a consistent, sustained manner, in their own time, with their own strategy they completed the task.

Make *prayatna* a principle. If you say that you have put a

lot of effort into a solution, it means you are ignoring this law. When you experience that flow, you will enjoy work. Whenever you can say, "I enjoy my work," it shows you are in a playful mood. When you enjoy your work, you don't aggravate stress. With very little energy, you can accomplish anything. If you don't enjoy your work, how will you accomplish your goals? Despite your sweat and toil, the results will still be negligible. No one will appreciate you, either. An intelligent person, who puts a little effort in an ingenious way, is appreciated by the whole world. Another individual works very hard but doesn't experience this flow, and the world fails to recognize him.

Yoga Nidra: *Vishnu's "Sleep"*

Let us see how Lord Vishnu applied the *Law of Least Effort*. Vishnu is the Chief Executive of the entire universe, the one who maintains law and order. His staff is a very meager set of seven *rishis* and one *garuda*, (his chauffeur, the eagle), along with his wife and two gatekeepers. With 11 people, Vishnu manages the whole world. Since there are a lot of evil characters in the world, being in charge of the universe is quite a stressful job. But how does Vishnu manage? He reclines on his serpent bed, peacefully and comfortably. But don't think that he is asleep; Vishnu is very alert. He is in *yoga nidra* – thought-free awareness. He is very quiet, not reacting to anything. Though he is facing the complex problems of the world, maintaining balance and order, Vishnu is quietly lying down without any thought agitations in his mind. As he watches, problems arise, and, bringing their own solutions, solve themselves. There is no need to interfere. If you interfere, you add to the whole, complex problem. When problems appear in your life, they also bring their own solution. You must allow the problem to solve itself. That is what Naturopathy practitioners claim, "If there is a fever, there is a reason for it. Perhaps you need to cleanse some toxins from the body."

Vishnu only watches, without any thought agitation. In our case, when a problem arises, thought agitations follow. The problem swallows you up; you don't know how to solve it. Instead of allowing that, stand apart; quietly observe the problem. Let the problem solve itself. When you allow the problem to solve itself, you spend the least energy and the problem is resolved. If you try to poke your nose into the problem, you create more difficulties for yourself and others. Patiently wait, and watch, 90 % of your problems will simply disappear.

Early in the morning you are awakened by a phone call and learn that there is a problem at the office. "My boss is very angry. He is searching for a certain file, and he is unable to trace it." With great trepidation, you rush to the office. On the way you swallow a tablet to calm your nervousness. However, once you reach the office, there are no signs of any difficulty! Your boss apologizes, "I'm sorry for troubling you. I found the file I was looking for in *my* drawer." The problem is solved. But, in between, our peace of mind was completely disturbed, our heartbeat raced, and blood pressure rose. What remains are our physiological problems. The rest of the problem is solved. Any problem that comes also brings a solution. The solution to a problem is like a bud that blossoms into a flower. A problem provides an opportunity ... for you to watch!

Patiently watching problems solve themselves is what is called effortless playfulness. Rather than dissipating your psychological and physical energy, you conserve the energy and can easily resolve the remaining 10% of the problem. Conserve your energy and apply that conserved energy in solving genuine problems. Most of the time, we fight against non-existing issues. We fight phony, phantom problems. The more you fight against them, the more wounds you accumulate. What is there to fight against? The biggest problem is your imagination! Those who follow the *Law of Least Effort* relax when a problem comes. Like the Namboodri's tale of woe – "My wife fell into the well, and our house is on fire!" Then he pause and sighs, "I'll chew some *paan* and think about it a while." Relax a little, like Vishnu lies down and yet is in charge of the whole universe. There is a solution for every problem.

Taking Vishnu's Example

At Sabarmati Ashram in Ahmedabad, India, there is a room in which Mahatma Gandhi worked. The room is maintained in the same state as it was during Gandhi's time. If you were to go there, you would observe just one seat, a kind of folded thick cloth on which Gandhi used to sit, a small table, his pen and reading glasses. On another side of the room is Gandhi's *charkha*, and his *chappals* in another corner. This is all that he owned. And with this meager equipment, staff and assistance, he ran the whole struggle for independence. You and I require seven steno-typists, computers, an air-conditioned office, wall-to-wall carpeting, piped-in music, and a periodic supply of caffeine-laden soda pop – and still we are not able to manage! But Gandhi in his simplicity, with his meager means and relaxed effort, handled the whole of it.

Gandhi had this enormous power to move effortlessly from one situation to another. While working on the *charkha* (spinning wheel) he is concentrating deeply and intensely; nothing distracts him – no political problem, no social problem, nothing! After half an hour spinning is over, as he sets his spinning wheel aside, someone thrusts a child into Gandhi's hands. He picks up that child, plays and talks small talk, making the child giggle, and then hands the child back to his caretakers. Following that small interlude, he drives away to the most crucial meeting – either with the Viceroy or the Congress Working Committee. There, he is a totally different person. By evening, he is preparing for the prayer meeting. Thereafter, setting aside everything else, he is ready to serve a leper who came to his *ashram*, washing his wounds and speaking kind words to him. Finally, at nine o'clock he goes to bed and sleeps well.

If you or I were to go to bed at 9 o'clock, we would never sleep. We would toss and turn, look at the ceiling, watch TV for some time, check out what is in the refrigerator, have a glass of milk and one biscuit and return to bed. Still you would not be sleepy. You turn the TV on again, flip the channels and turn it off again. This way we spent the whole night in frivolous activity, and in the morning we wake up with heavy eyelids and feeling very frustrated, agitated, and lacking the energy and enthusiasm to even get out of bed!

This is how we spend our time, whereas Gandhi worked effortlessly, yet he never lacked energy. He moved from one theatre of activity to another with maximum ease, without any effort. Whether it is Gandhi or Vishnu, we find them following the *Law of Least Effort.* When you think you are making more effort, pause and think: "Am I on the right track?" When you feel you are tired, pause and question: "Am I on the right track?" You may think, "I am the only person who does all the work in this house. I am tired, over-worked and too busy to have time for anything else!" This means that you may be utilizing your energy unintelligently. A busy person finds time for anything and everything. A lazy man has time for no one and nothing.

Vishnu provides a wonderful example and solution, relaxed and poised in *yoga nidra,* with a calm and a contemplative consciousness, he relates to all the world's problems. This way, problems will become the opportunity for unfolding your potential.

Pauranic Examples

Krishna had to tackle the problem of Kaliyan, the invisible, menacing serpent, who terrorized the people of Vrindavan, and hid himself in the Jamuna River. The Jamuna itself has blackish water, and Kaliyan is still blacker. Like the Taliban, who for a long time were operating without the larger public noticing, no one was aware of the serpent, Kaliyan, who was swimming invisibly in the Jamuna waters. Kaliyan was prospering in the Jamuna but had poisoned the water. No one understood the seriousness of the problem, until two cows that drank the river water just collapsed. Another bull also died after drinking from the Jamuna. People then understood the seriousness of the problem.

Later, they saw hot fumes emerging from the river. Still, no one could pinpoint the exact problem. Then Krishna jumped into the water, and Kaliyan immediately raised his seven hoods and stood threateningly, towering over Krishna. Krishna jumped on Kaliyan's head and performed a dance – right there! Hood after hood, Kaliyan became tired, and, ultimately, he had to pray to Krishna, "Please spare me! Please forgive and release me! I lay at your feet." For Krishna, the whole thing was a dance – not a fight – only a dance. Similarly, an intelligent person can convert even a fight into an experience of dance. Krishna gave a great teaching for us, demonstrating how to playfully solve a problem. This playful way is the right way, the easiest way and the spiritual way of problem solving. If you are under stress, your energies are suppressed. If you are stress free then infinite energy is available to you. Then, alone, does one become playful.

Because Krishna came into this world to solve mankind's problems in a playful manner, his manifestation has specially been named "*Leelavatara*." Kamsa sent Putana to kill baby Krishna by breastfeeding him with her poisonous milk. Krishna sucked her milk as well as her blood. In the process, Putana, the would-be-killer, was herself killed. Krishna drew a solution from the problem itself.

Once, Krishna fought with the cruel King of Magadha, Jarasanda, who had assembled a huge army. Krishna knew that there is no point in fighting head-on, so he withdrew from the battlefield. Everyone laughed, but it was a very successful military strategy. When Jarasanda's army finally came deep into the inner territory, Krishna attacked and destroyed them.

Playfulness is the best form of problem-solving. Wherever you have to withdraw, do so. Wherever you have to lay low, use that tactic. Wherever you need to assert, then assert, and whenever you have to advance, adopt that strategy. This playful approach becomes a dance. Your nimble-footedness, felicity and energy are capable of tackling any problem. Others may busily consult a book and apply whatever is written there. But the pity is, a book only describes old, known situations and rarely new ones. Better to apply one's ingenuity, one's intelligence and understanding to the problems of life.

Once, Rama was to fight with Vali, the Monkey King. No one dared to fight Vali, because anybody who did would be robbed of half his energy. Rama had to search for a new solution to this problem, determine the right kind of *prayatna* instead of adopting some head-on collision course. Thus, Rama hid himself behind the trees (an illegal tactic in the ordinary course of combat) and from this position was able to strike Vali, without confronting him face to face, and very effortlessly solved the problem.

These are several instances that we find in our Indian Pauranic tradition where intelligence brings new solutions and energy to solving a problem. When you bring the same old energy, it is very boring. New solutions and energy are a very exciting experience. The play or *leela* makes life very interesting.

Pauranic Problem Solving

There is nothing to be serious about in life. Seriousness is madness. Whenever we look at some problem, we become very serious and all the avenues of creativity in us become blocked. Unable to bring that energy of playfulness in our life, we lose all ability to solve life's problems. How can you experience the flow of energy? This law is to be applied religiously and deliberately. Mere understanding is not enough. That is what we see in all the experience of the *Pauranic* masters – whether Rama, Krishna or other *avataras*. They came into this world to face and play out problems, and to teach mankind.

Vamana, the fifth *avatara* of Vishnu had to tackle Mahabali who was a very *dharmic* king. But the only problem with Mahabali was that he was an atheist. Atheism is the highest form of arrogance. In the material world such people perform perfectly, but inside they are deeply arrogant and their whole outer perfection becomes a burden for them. Their arrogance becomes crystallized in the process. The Lord thought, "This is not the way my devotee should function in this world," so the Lord decided to remove Mahabali's arrogance. The Lord came in the form of a Vamana and asked for a small thing: "Give me three feet of land."

This method was simple and effortless, so no one suspected anything. That is what we now call "low tech, high concept." The technology used is very simple, but the concept is very sophisticated. So Vamana came in the guise of a Brahmin boy and asked Bali, for three feet of land. Mahabali allotted Vamana this modest request. Once the promise was given, Vamana suddenly transformed himself into a huge figure. With one foot, he measured earth, another foot he measured heaven, because Mahabali had been ruling both heaven and earth with his power. Then Vamana asked Bali, "Where will I put my third foot?" And Mahabali, understood and humbly replied, "My Lord, place it on my head." Thus Vamana placed his foot on Mahabali's head, and the king was pushed underground. The idea is that his ego was demolished in a very peaceful, useful and easy way. You find that all the *avataras* are very playful in their approach to problem-solving, let it be Krishna, Rama, Vamana or Narasimha.

Hiranya Kasibu constantly abused his son, Prahlada. There was no ordinary solution for this problem. When one's protector turns into a perpetrator of crime, it is a time when the Lord's manifestation appears. Prahlada always chanted, "Hare Rama, Hare Krishna." But Hiranya Kasibu wanted him to chant, "Hare Hiranya; Wealth is God; Greed is God," Prahlada refused, so Hiranya became very angry and tortured him in many ways.

Then came the day, while Prahlada was uttering a prayer, Hiranya chided him: "Where is your god, now?" Prahlada replied, "He is everywhere." Then Hiranya mockingly asked, "Is he in this pillar?" Prahlada said, "Yes!" Hearing Prahlada's defiant answer infuriated Hiranya, and he struck the pillar so forcefully that it split. Out came a half lion, half man, Narasimha, the man-lion *avatara*, and grabbed Hiranya, pinioned him across his lap, slit open his stomach, pulled out his intestines, drank his blood and roared a mighty roar. In an instant, the problem was solved. Then Prahlada cried again,

"O Lord, please resume your peaceful form," and the half-lion, half-human obeyed.

God is Fun

Study any story of great people. They have this ability to bring fresh energy into the whole process of problem-solving. They appear to be effortless. This experience can be encapsulated in a single sentence: "An intelligent person *enjoys* a problem." When you enjoy what you are doing, then you operate on a level where plenty of energy is available to you. Thus, one should learn to enjoy whatever one is doing – that is, to "have fun." Someone said, "God is fun." – that is, when you enjoy, you are God. If you are relaxed, then the very exercise of solving the problem is an enjoyable experience, self-discovery – fun!

You may be heading in an army unit to the terrorist-infested borders of Kashmir, but your friend remarks, "Have fun." Whatever you are doing, "Have a nice time!" This attitude is to be cultivated. Happiness should not be postponed. We always delay, thinking, "I will be happy tomorrow," chasing a mirage. When we were students we thought that when we completed our education, happiness would dawn. Were we happy after that? Then we thought we would be happy once we found a job. Were we happy then? Then we thought, "After marriage." On and on it goes. When are you going to be happy? If you want to be happy, decide to be happy right now! That is why it is said, happiness is here and now. If you postpone it, you will never be happy.

Happiness is playfulness. You don't need to change your situation, people's opinions or the environment, your stars or the constellations in the heavens. Only *you* are responsible for your happiness, so decide right now, as you are! That is the supreme act of spiritual intelligence. When you decide to be happy, thereafter you will no longer work *for* happiness. When you work to *attain* happiness, your work becomes a big burden because you always think, "Today I am unhappy, and tomorrow I will be happy." Consequently, all the time you are unhappy. Therefore you have to decide to be happy right now, as you are, and then go about doing everything happily. That is the meaning of playfulness.

When you happily go about doing things, problems can be easily solved, because you have a happy mind. When you bring an unhappy mind, you only compound the problems that you face. Decide to be happy. Attune to the *Law of Playfulness.*

Don't create any gap between yourself, your activities, your aspirations and your happiness. That gap is merely psychological and the source of all problems. To close that gap is the loftiest intelligence. When we decide to be happy right away, then problems disappear and become opportunities. One encounters that flow experience. Once that flow experience comes, the entire experience of Spirit is available to you for tackling all life's problems. The act of suddenly discovering the source of your happiness as your own self comes as a blessing. Once you discover and develop that intelligence, life thereafter is a dance – a very happy and blissful experience.

Pulling it all Together

This discovery is what is most important and it requires immense intelligence. Without that intelligence, it is not possible. To have playfulness of life, we have to employ all other Spiritual Laws governing life and its quality. Realize that you are that *Field of Infinite Potentialities*, and that you are a unique individual. Everything in life changes with that understanding of the law of Your Uniqueness. Know, also, the *Law of Change* or *Maya* – that everything is constantly changing. The *Law of Dharma* declares that you have a mission in this world, which you must discover and develop. You must also know the *Law of Karma*, that you are responsible for your deeds; no one else is to blame. Thus, you have the inner resources to choose your responses to situations and live in accordance with the *Law of Yajna*, or *The Law of Sacrifice*. Finally, applying the *Law of Yoga*, live the life of *Detachment*. Once you apply these six Spiritual Laws, you will understand the seventh law, the *Law of Least Effort*, *Leela* or *Playfulness* – that a highly accomplished person is the most relaxed person. A very busy person has time for everything! Such was the message that both Vishnu and Krishna gave.

There is a wonderful statement depicting *Shiva Tandava* quoted in a work written by Dr. S. Radhakrishnan, "*Jagathrayam sambavanartano stali natadhi rajotra parasivasvayam / sabha nata ranga iti vyavasthitih / swarooptatah saktiyutat prayuktathah*:" "The three worlds are the dancing halls of Sambava Shiva, the Lord of the Dance; and the wonder is that Shiva himself has become the hall, the dance, the dancer and the spectators!" Shiva has only two modes of existence: either he is meditating, imperturbable, calm and quiet, or he is dancing, engaged in graceful, effortless movement of energy. When Shiva dances – his creative enterprise – he creates the world. Dance means the effortless flow of energy. Whether you are teaching, cooking, cleaning the house, driving, working in the office or in the army, wherever you are, experience this flowing energy. Be like Shiva – effortless, relaxed; and like Krishna, always smiling.

The Unbidden Smile

The ultimate experience of the *Law of Least Effort* is that you are smiling person. If you cannot smile, then take up smiling as a personal discipline. Patanjali includes the "*yoga* of smiling" in his *Yoga Sutras*. This *yoga* can be practiced! Every morning go to the *puja* room, look in the mirror and draw the corners of your mouth towards your ears. When you try this *yogic* exercise for ten minutes, you will automatically smile and be relaxed. The ultimate expression of relaxation is your ability to smile.

If you can smile without any motive, that is, without seeking something from someone, then your smile is a spiritual smile. Otherwise your smile is purposeful and devious, harboring a motive. The spiritual smile is motiveless. It is an expression of your natural bliss. Once you discover that your happiness does not depend upon any situation, for the first time, there is a spontaneous smile and easiness, an experience of wellness.

Thereafter, under all conditions – "*Yogarato vaa bhogarato vaa / sangarato vaa sangaviheenah / yasya brahmani ramate chittam / nandati nandati nandatyeva*" (*Bhaja Govindam*. 18). "Whether you are in the company of people, or isolated, whether you are in the forest or in the midst of civilization, rich or poor, a success or failure, whether you are ill or well, it does not matter! You are continuously in that blissful state of experience and have enormous energy at your disposal." This is the ultimate meaning of playfulness.

Prerequisites to Playfulness

Now we come to a point of very technical advice: in order to make life a playful experience, a very relaxed and easy flow of energy, the first thing one has to develop is some skill for which you have a natural disposition. You have to develop your inborn natural skills. Otherwise you cannot be relaxed. Suppose you want to be a musician. The first key to leading a relaxed, happy, fulfilled life as a musician is to develop skill in music. If you have no skills as a musician, no disposition or natural inclination towards music, singing songs will be painful for you – and listening to your singing will be a pain for others! Once you discover your natural inclination, develop it. Develop skills and pursue them with consistency and constancy.

The second requirement is to have a range of interests. You are not a horse with blinkers on your eyes, just plodding along towards your destination. Have many interests – music, mathematics, politics, poetry, science, etc. When you have a range of interests, you can look at issues from a multi-dimensional perspective. From such a broad standpoint, you can bring this range of interests into your pursuits. This means having a global vision. Though your activities may be local, you have a readiness to incorporate many perspectives. Then act according to the need of the moment, responding to situations as they emerge. When you have a global vision and a local response, you access the intelligence of Spirit, and the invisible energies of Spirit start unfolding. Your *kundalini* will arise. When *kundalini* arises, your inner energies arise unhindered in a state of continuous ecstasy.

Lord Krishna says, "Arjuna, I have already won this battle for you," meaning, "be effortless" (*Gita.* 11: 33). "Don't have any hesitation; please believe in what I say. Have that faith and go to war." Whenever we undertake an activity, go with this confidence: "I have already won this battle. Let there be no hesitation whatsoever." When you move into the battlefield with that faith, determination and understanding, victory is certain. "*Tasmat tvam uttistha yaso labhasva / jitva satrun bhunksva rajyam samrddham / may'avi aite nihatah purvam eva / nimitta-matram bhava savyasacin*" (*Gita*. 11:33). "O Arjuna, arise! Destroy your enemies and enjoy a prosperous kingdom. These warriors have already been slain by Me. May you be my instrument alone." You become only an instrument. That is all that we have to do. When we have that attitude of being an instrument in the hands of this Infinite Intelligence, thereafter, life experience is a constant flow – a flow of limitless energy. Experiencing that limitless energy in all our activities is the meaning of effortless action.

This spontaneity will not come simply by analysis. The more one analyzes, the more paralyzed one becomes, because that mode of intelligence is not enough. Bringing an ethical sensitivity into your analytical skill is what is required. Ethics give the light of wisdom and will assist you in solving most of your problems. In addition to your ethical sensitivity a spiritual foundation is requisite. Otherwise, you may be ethical, but you will still be miserable; your good work will become a prison-house without a spiritual foundation for your deeds.

All your analytical and problem-solving skills are to be conditioned by ethical sensitivity and a spiritual foundation. Spiritually rooted, ethically sensitive and prepared as a highly skilled, problem-solving individual, you enjoy life's *leela*.

The ultimate spiritual experience is your ability to solve a problem and make decisions "situationally." Decision-making is the expression of your clarity. If you cannot act spontaneously, then you are not spiritual. If you need to say, "Give me a week and I will think about it," in such an instance, you will never decide. As problems unfold, as the kaleidoscopically changing world brings problems and issues before you, can you respond in a split second, taking into consideration all aspects of the problem.

Spontaneity is the final flowering of our spirituality. Not stuck anywhere, constantly flowing – these are the most important bases of spirituality. When we have to ponder, we abide in fear and anxiety and finally say, "I have postponed the decision-making." The highest achievement of spiritual expression is one's ability to spontaneously respond to situations. If you are rooted in your spiritual fullness and your ethical sensitivity, able to respond to situations spontaneously, that is the highest art of living. That will give you the "flow experience" – what the *Law of Least Effort* means. Effortlessly you move about, like a lion that roars – his whole body effortlessly participates in that roar. When his whole body participates in the roar, the whole of nature spontaneously cooperates with him. Or, like a lion that leaps upon a galloping antelope. Waiting for its prey, he remains absolutely motionless. The lion does not gawk here and there, pondering what the future will bring. The lion's whole energy is concentrated, springs at the antelope in a split second, tackles and devours it.

That kind of a spontaneous movement is something like what happens when you suddenly step on a snake. What do you do? Pause and say, "Let me ask my *guru*. Should I leap away or not?" When you see that you are about to step on a snake, you immediately jump, don't you? Or what do you do when your house is on fire? You leap out without thinking. No one has to persuade you. Your response is a spontaneous activity.

When your spontaneity awakens, there is no hesitation, deliberation is integrated effortlessly. Your responses are spontaneous, instantaneous, and natural. Such a person never stops anywhere, never strikes roots. Over time, most of us become bogged down with inertia, no energy to move. But an enlightened person is constantly on the move, and, the more he moves, the more he enjoys spontaneity and the more his energies awaken.

This is the final state of supreme, spiritual unfoldment. Spontaneous and playful, nothing holds you back. In that movement, there is no noise, no sound, no effort or friction, like an evening star appearing in the night sky and taking its place in the order of things. Or like the sun rising on the horizon without any noise, like a flower blooming or dew descending upon blades of grass, or the morning sun licking up the trembling dew – there is no noise, only a state of total relaxation, and peace and supreme creativity.

This is the ultimate destiny of human intelligence – to achieve that state of total spontaneity, playfulness and creativity, deriving moment-to-moment responses to all challenging situations. That is your privilege, your birthright, your destiny, and mission in this world. May God bless you to move unto that platform of ecstasy and experience life as a play of Consciousness.

Epilogue

From Ignorance to Enlightenment

This great movement from *bandha* to *moksa*, from bondage to liberation, from *samsara* to *nirvana*, from ignorance to enlightenment, is determined by these seven Universal Spiritual Laws – laws discovered by the ancient *rishis* and compiled in Hindu scripture. Presently, we are uncomfortable with ourselves and our circumstances. We want to be free; we want to be unconditionally happy. All of us desire Self-unfoldment. This sense of discomfort with who we are, what we are, and falling short of our Self-fulfillment, makes us restless. How is it that we may achieve that miracle, moving from a life of limitation to a life of limitless possibilities?

We know that in discovering and following the world's physical laws we have been able to lift ourselves – in a material sense – from deplorable poverty and inhuman suffering. By following moral laws, we are capable both of creating a harmonious civil society and of enhancing the quality of our interactive lives. Still we are un-free; we are bound. Fear thrives. Tension and violence transpire between us. We have not really discovered that *true* freedom. To discover that freedom and to gain true satisfaction, limitless joy and bliss, one is to follow these seven Hindu Spiritual Laws.

To eliminate suffering and improve our lives, we have to understand each of these laws and rigorously apply them. If you ignore the laws of the community or country in which you live, you will end up in prison. Even if you plead ignorance of the law, you will still end up in prison. Similarly, if you don't follow the physical laws of this universe, the result will be self-inflicted harm and suffering. Ignorance of the law is not an excuse – "Oh, no one told me; I never knew!" Then, for your ignorance, you will suffer. And suffering will slowly educate you. Suffering will slowly nudge you into understanding the law. Failure to implement these spiritual laws increases your suffering and all opportunity for abiding happiness is lost.

It is only when all these seven *Hindu Spiritual Laws* are fully understood that one comes to know the collective significance of these laws. To understand each law fully, you must also understand the other laws and their interconnectedness. In their mutual proximity, each law reveals more and more of its depth and meaning.

A Disciplined Pursuit

To apply these seven universal Spiritual Laws, certain discipline is involved. For example, a moral law – such as not telling lies – is sometimes very difficult to apply. As a youth, you may have stolen money from your father's billfold. But, when your father came and shouted – "Who took my money?" – no one dared say a word. When he asked you directly, "Did you take my money?" you meekly responded, "No," telling a lie and narrowly escaping your father's wrath. Did you really escape from that situation? On the contrary! No, you did not, because you failed to follow a moral law. With every lie you tell, your tendency to tell another lie increases. Later on a situation will arise when you are caught with the full blast of accumulated effects. Then you pay the *full* price of all your past misdeeds.

Not to lie, or steal or kill – these are some of the moral laws that, if we follow, enhance the quality of our lives. But, because we are always more motivated by immediate rewards and results, we often don't bother to follow these laws. We are unable to restrain that impulse, slow down our reactions and make the right choices.

To move from a state of consciousness steeped in suffering to a state of consciousness filled with continuous joy, happiness and fulfillment, we have only to follow the Spiritual Laws we have discussed. Discipline is the price one must pay in this (or in any) pursuit.

In an organized civil society, the price is civic discipline. You cannot legally toss your garbage on the road if you live in an organized, civil society. The urge to toss refuse on the roadside, or jump a red light – or break any law of the land – is curbed by inner discipline, by sacrificing for the benefit of the common good. When a stoplight suddenly turns red, you apply the brakes and stop your car. But your immediate impulse may have been just the opposite. The thought flashed through your mind, "No one is around to notice. I can jump this light." Ultimately, such a habit creates chaos. By restraining our individual impulses, we improve our lives – individually *and* collectively. So, too, as we pursue our fulfillment through the application of these seven spiritual laws, certain curbs upon our impulses are required.

Seven Steps to Self-Actualization

To uplift ourselves from our present condition of spiritual poverty, of ignorance and limitations, of *duhkha* or suffering, in order to realize our full potential, to have the experience of growth, of learning, expanding and encompassing the whole universe, it is vital that as individuals we understand these spiritual laws *and* apply them. That is what is known as Self-Unfoldment, Self-Realization, or Self-Actualization (the term which the western World has adopted).

Self-Actualization is the experience of expansion. We all want that movement because we are unhappy as we are today. We want that quantum leap, that metamorphosis, that miracle to happen. We want freedom; we want to be happy, and we cannot afford any compromise. Follow these seven *Spiritual Laws* and tap into the field of *Infinite Potentialities.*